PRAISE FOR *His Last Resort*

"Captivating! Riveting! An excellently crafted storyline that adroitly and profoundly expresses the struggles to understand God's will and to live according to His principles. You did it again, M. A. Malcolm!" — Tracia

"… a page turner. Good, clean romance. It delves into the word of God in a way that is relatable to everyday living. The issues are real, it's not just fiction. In my opinion it is a must-have in any book lover's collection. Appreciated in today's society of moral decline." — Marsha C.

"This was my first time reading a Christian romance… and I thoroughly enjoyed the vivid way it was written. There were times I felt the characters were my friends. The book also encourages introspection, which I loved." — Rochelle

"This masterpiece is a testimony that God doesn't only use preachers to share the word…. I have truly been blessed by reading this powerful story. God has spoken and readers will be truly blessed by the entire book." — Nichole

"*His Last Resort* is a reminder that this is a changing world, and the Lord has been changing His tactics for filling His Kingdom. He uses His most creative methods to save us through His Son, Jesus Christ. He comes down to our level and uses the very unconventional methods, gifts and talents so all of us have the opportunity to have eternal life." — Robin

HIS LAST

RESORT

A Contemporary Christian Romance

M. A. Malcolm

HIS LAST RESORT
Copyright © 2017 M. A. Malcolm
All rights reserved.
Published by M. A. Malcolm, 2017
Westmoreland, Jamaica.

Books may be purchased by contacting the publisher/author directly. For more information, please visit authormamalcolm.com.

All Scripture quotations, unless otherwise noted, are taken from the MODERN ENGLISH VERSION (MON): Centenary Translation: THE NEW TESTAMENT IN MODERN ENGLISH by Helen Barrett Montgomery, 1924.

Scriptures marked NKJV are taken from the NEW KING JAMES VERSION (NKJV): Scripture taken from the NEW KING JAMES VERSION®. Copyright© 1982 by Thomas Nelson, Inc. Used by permission. All rights reserved.

Author's photo: Kiffa Davis Photography (kiffadavis@outlook.com)
Cover design: Helen Evans (www.fiverr.com/helenevans)
           & Nitpicking with a Purpose (nitpickingwithapurpose.com)
Cover images: bst2012/depositphotos.com & jbryson/depositphotos.com
Editing: Amy Vanhorn (amyevanhorn@gmail.com)
Formatting Nitpicking with a Purpose (nitpickingwithapurpose.com)
Writing consultant: Terri Whitmire (www.thewriterstablet.org)

ISSN 0799-494X (Print)   ISBN 978-976-95815-5-5 (Paperback)
ISSN 0799-4958 (Mobi)   ISBN 978-976-95815-6-2 (eBook)
ISSN 0799-4965 (ePub)

Printed in the United States of America by CreateSpace.
First Printing, March 2017

For every reader who asked for more.

A Note from the Author

Thank you so much for choosing *His Last Resort*! If you're familiar with my writing, then you've no doubt read my debut novel, *His Last Hope*, which I released in 2015.

His Last Hope was expected to be my only attempt at fiction, but the readers just weren't having it! In response to reader requests, I now present *His Last Resort*, Book One in the *His Last Hope Series*, and the prequel to *His Last Hope*. It is a standalone story that takes place several years <u>before</u> the main action of *His Last Hope*.

As the story you're about to read is unfolding, the fictional town of Alistair Bay, which is the setting of *His Last Hope*, is just a concept in the mind of the real estate developers. Facebook, YouTube and Spotify are still unheard of, and people are listening to CD players and MP3's. Smartphones aren't nearly as popular as they are now, and communication is a little more difficult than it is in the 'real' world of today.

I hope the story of Robert Marsden and Claire Foxwood blesses you and brings a smile to your face.

Your beauty should not come from outward adornment, such as elaborate hairstyles and the wearing of gold jewelry or fine clothes. Rather, it should be that of your inner self, the unfading beauty of a gentle and quiet spirit, which is of great worth in God's sight.

1 Peter 3:3-4 (NKJV)

CHAPTER ONE

Claire Foxwood was a walking contradiction who had mastered the art of pretending to be something she wasn't. She figured, based on people's response to her, that she did a good job of convincing people she was confident and always 'together'—whatever that meant. Only those closest to her knew that she really wasn't all that confident, and she was almost never completely 'together.'

Inside, she was still the chubby middle schooler whose mother had entered her into countless beauty contests in order to get her out of the shell she was building around herself with books. By sixteen, she still hadn't emerged from that shell, but she knew how to take deep breaths and tamp down the voice of self-doubt in her head long enough to make a few turns on the runway. Once she got under those stage lights, she could *work it* like her life depended on it, but off-stage, she was a pool of insecurity.

Inside, she was still the overweight high school student who—despite being able to command a stage as a model—stuttered her way through her valedictory speech. Whose idea was it to declare that the student with the highest GPA had to give a speech anyway? Who assumed that getting good grades translated into the ability to speak without stumbling over every third word? She had learned how to strut her stuff, but put a microphone in front of her, and she had no idea what to do with it.

Inside, she was still the over-achieving high school graduate defending herself to people who didn't understand that she *still* didn't know what she wanted to be when she grew up. She had to explain over and over why she was the valedictorian with no college scholarship. When she was asked, she had to admit that she hadn't even *applied* to college. She already knew, even then, that the things she wanted to learn weren't always taught in lecture rooms.

The good news was that by the time she was twenty-six or so, Claire Foxwood had more or less figured out what she wanted to be when she grew up. She wanted to be someone who helped other people to feel better about themselves than she felt about herself. She wasn't sure how she was going to do that, but she knew she'd only brushed the surface in her job as a receptionist at an insurance company.

Even disgruntled clients spent a few extra minutes with her at the front desk, and her boss knew that she was responsible for a lot of the repeat business the company experienced. When she applied for a job as an assistant underwriter in the same office, her manager explained that while they had no doubt about her abilities, she was most valuable exactly where she was. At least they compensated her well, and she was able to save her annual bonuses for the five years she worked there.

She didn't need a university education to know that she really had no scope for advancement in the company. At the same time, she understood that filling people up with compliments that made them stand taller and smile wider didn't pay the bills. Eventually, she turned her fascination with makeup—developed as she watched her beloved grandmother transform her face with various products—into a vocation. She gained certification in makeup artistry and applied for a job at the makeup counter in the nearest mall. After taking night classes at the local community college, she graduated with an associate degree in business and was able to use five years' worth of savings as the capital she needed to open her own small makeup store, which she named Outside-In.

Despite becoming a business owner, Claire still knew that she needed a major dose of self-confidence, and she still knew that she didn't have it all 'together.' She was just glad that the rest of the world hadn't figured it out yet. Every day, she would apply a mask from the inside out so she could interact with her clients and help them to become more confident than she was. Even so, she still resided inside a fiction-lined shell to which she escaped after work every day.

CßMurray

Claire knew she had a lot to be grateful for. Being a small business owner was no small feat. After a year of doing everything herself, she'd finally been able to hire a shop assistant whom she had taught everything she knew before paying for her to do the same makeup artistry course Claire had completed a couple of years before. She no longer had to be at the store from the moment it opened until it closed. She was finally able to take the odd day off, and she left work at two o'clock every Wednesday and every other Saturday unless she had an appointment. Her little company also offered in-home services for special events like weddings and high school proms.

She treasured her 'me-time' immensely. Everyone in her inner circle understood that you simply didn't call Claire on her Wednesday afternoons off; unscheduled visits were a definite 'no-no.'

The Wednesday-afternoon-off side of her still felt like the little girl who would rather get lost among the pages of a book than set one foot outside her house. This was the side of Claire that couldn't wait to get home to the little rented bungalow she shared with her German shepherd Chaz. There, she was quite content to don a stocking cap, remove all the make-up and slip into a warm bath. She would turn on the mp3 player that hardly ever left its place on the bathroom counter and listen to worship music or dramatized audio versions of her favorite books—Agatha Christie's masterful works of fiction.

Bath time was an inalterable Wednesday-afternoon-off ritual. She would remove her contact lenses, strip down, wrap herself in a bath robe, and give her achy feet or shoulders a quick massage before sliding into water scented with her favorite essential oil. Then she would lounge in the tub until the water cooled, and Chaz would relax at his special spot between the tub and the bidet that hadn't been used since she had moved in.

It was therefore no surprise that she was lying in the tub listening to Dame Christie's *The Mirror Crack'd from Side to Side* when Chaz jumped up and ran barking towards the front door as the doorbell rang at around six-thirty. Claire didn't move. She never got visits from people who didn't call first, and she wasn't expecting any deliveries. Whoever it was obviously had the wrong address.

The doorbell rang a second time and then a third, with Chaz barking loudly all the while, before she finally got out of the bath, wrapped herself in a fluffy yellow bath robe, put on steamed-up glasses she could barely see out of, and plodded towards the front of the house. If she got there and it was somebody offering her a religious tract, she just might lose her own religion all over them. How annoying!

She opened the front door and through the screen and foggy lenses noticed a small cardboard box on the welcome mat. The man who had placed it there was halfway down the porch steps when he turned around and the two of them made eye contact through the screen.

It wasn't immediately clear whether it would turn out to be good or bad, but as soon as her eyes met his, Claire knew without a shadow of a doubt that her destiny was somehow linked to this man she'd never laid eyes on before.

CHAPTER TWO

Robert Marsden almost laughed out loud when he saw the spectacle that came to the door. He quickly tried to remember the date, but decided it was either too early or too late for Halloween. The person standing there bore a striking resemblance to a beloved television character that was big, fluffy and yellow all over. His gaze quickly traveled up from the burgundy-tipped toes to the robe that almost brushed the floor and the mismatched, bright orange belt hastily tied around the waist. His eyes finally settled on the slightly parted lips forming an 'O' of surprise. He forced himself to pull his gaze away from the pink mouth and look into the eyes—make that thick glasses—the shower-cap wearing woman who was staring at him as if trying to memorize his face.

"M-m-may I help you?" She stuttered.

"Yes. I'm looking for Mrs. Claire Foxwood." He tried, no doubt unsuccessfully, to hide his amusement.

The woman pulled the lapels of her robe closer together, her other arm holding the knot in the belt. He wondered if she was afraid the robe would unexpectedly leap off her body and assault the screen door separating them. The German Shepherd beside her remained standing, although it had finally stopped barking.

"Well, you've found her. And it's *Miss* Foxwood. How may I be of assistance?"

"My name is Robert Marsden, *Miss* Foxwood, and I'm from the Notes in the Margin bookstore in town. I'm sure you're familiar with it?" His words started out as a statement but ended up as a question. Surely this person didn't go out in public!

"Very." The one-word answer was a bit abrupt, but it was understandable; it was obvious that Robert had caught her at a bad time. Maybe *all* her times were bad times, judging from the frown that seemed to be permanently etched into what he could see of her countenance. The woman's glasses seemed to take up half her face. He wondered again if she ever left the confines of her home.

He imagined she was the kind of woman who didn't have many friends… the kind of woman who spent quite a bit of her work day on the telephone… the kind of woman who used books as a means of escaping her mundane life.

"I'm sorry to turn up without calling first, but the telephone number you gave us is out of order, so I thought I'd just swing by with this." He waved in the direction of the box he had left on the mat.

CB

Claire winced as she remembered accidentally tripping over the telephone jack and pulling it right out of the wall. It had been a couple of days, but she hadn't remembered to get it fixed.

"What is it?" She looked down at the box through the screen door she still hadn't opened.

"Your prize." He smiled, revealing a row of perfect white teeth.

"Say what, now?" She was confused. It was hard to stop focusing on the man's handsome face long enough to hear what he was saying.

"You filled out an entry card at the bookstore recently, and you were the lucky winner."

She vaguely remembered dropping a card into a wire basket. "I don't believe in luck."

"Neither do I. Call it favor, then."

Claire's ears perked up. Was it possible that this fine specimen of a man was a believer? She quietly instructed her raging hormones to return to their corner before asking in a measured tone, "So, what was I highly favored enough to win?"

"A box of books. Twelve paperbacks from the three categories you selected on the card."

Now she remembered. She had selected cozy mystery, clean romance and Christian fiction.

"Congratulations, Mrs. Foxwood. I do hope you enjoy them, and that you'll encourage your friends to drop by Notes in the Margin. We run giveaways like this once every three months."

"Thank you."

As he moved away from the house, Claire noticed that there was no vehicle parked in her driveway. Instead, Robert Marsden took the walkway and turned right. She watched him until her view was blocked by the house next door. How was it possible that this man lived in her neighborhood and she wasn't even aware of him?

As she retrieved the box from the mat, she wondered how come she hadn't seen him in the bookstore before. It was roughly halfway between home and work. She'd been there several times, and she was impressed with the wide array of books they carried. What had drawn her attention even more was the fact that they didn't sell tabloid magazines or books with explicit content—a fact that was noted on a bulletin board close to the door. Instead, they carried shelf upon shelf of clean reading material, just the type Claire craved.

She placed the unopened box on the dining table and plodded back towards the bathroom, Chaz on her heels. She hoped the water hadn't cooled.

It hadn't.

She removed her glasses, dropped the robe, and stepped back into the tub. As the water covered her body, she reflected on her visits to the bookstore. Nope. She had never seen that man before; she would definitely remember if she had.

She leaned her head back onto the bath pillow and closed her eyes. There was something about him she couldn't put her finger on. Yes, he was attractive, but that wasn't quite it. Even through the screen door and the thick lenses, it was as if the man had looked right down into her soul and seen all her doubts and fears. It was as if every one of her insecurities were laid bare before him, though he'd barely spoken a few words to her. She had never experienced anything quite like it. She wondered if she would see him again.

Suddenly, she groaned and allowed herself to slide so deep into the water that her chin skimmed the bubbles. Eyes closed, she shook her head in regret. This man, who was quite possibly the man of her dreams—determined solely based on his good looks and use of the word 'favor'—had just seen her in her bath robe. The yellow one.

She sank a little deeper. Now her lips were under the bubbles.

The yellow bath robe that made her look like a rubber ducky. The one with the bright orange belt.

She held her breath as she sank all the way under, her feet sticking out of the water and resting on the either side of the faucet.

And her purple and aquamarine polka-dotted shower cap.

And her huge, thick glasses.

She sputtered and made her way back to the surface of the bubbles. She had, in all likelihood, just met the perfect man, and she could *not* have looked any worse!

CHAPTER THREE

For some reason she couldn't explain, Claire couldn't get Robert Marsden out of her mind. It had been years since she'd had a crush, and she couldn't understand what it was about the brief encounter that had caused her to feel so... *moved*.

There was nothing particularly special about him; at least, nothing she could have determined in the one or two minutes they had spent in each other's company.

She couldn't deny that he was attractive, with his smooth, dark skin and close-cropped hair. He was also well-spoken and was probably a Christian. All good things, surely. But what had struck her most was the way her very *spirit* had felt as if the atmosphere had shifted in the moment she had seen his face.

She couldn't describe it any other way.

She'd made eye contact with him, and her whole being had seemed to stop for just a moment. It was as if every last cell had stood at attention. And saluted.

The problem was that more than two weeks later, she still couldn't tell if what had happened was good or bad. She had prayed about it—like she prayed about everything that captured her attention—but still had no clarity.

So one Wednesday afternoon, curiosity finally got the better of her and she stopped at Notes in the Margin on her way home from work.

She sat in her car for a good five minutes, taking deep breaths and doing everything else she could think of to calm herself before stepping out. Then on her way to the bookstore, she caught a case of nerves and ducked into the coffee shop right next to it. Maybe if she ordered a brownie and a mango smoothie, they would help stabilize her blood sugar a little bit.

She lingered in the coffee shop until she drained the contents of the cup and ate every crumb of the double-chocolate treat.

Great. Now her blood sugar may be a bit too high.

She ordered a bottle of water and sat there sipping it. *Just to balance out all that sugar*, she told herself.

After several more minutes, she stood with determination. She had delayed as long as possible. It had been at least twenty-five minutes since she had shut her car engine off. It was now or never.

So she went into the bookstore. And there, as usual, was the older woman who manned the register. With no one else in sight, Claire waved hello, and the woman smiled in her direction. Now what was she supposed to do? In her mind's eye, Robert would have been within sight, and he would have recognized her and come over to say hi. She stood there looking around for a moment, but he was nowhere to be seen. Now what?

She headed towards one of her favorite shelves—cozy mystery—and dawdled there a bit, picking up a couple of titles from two of her preferred authors before stopping at the Christian fiction aisle, where she invariably spent most of her time on her visits to the store.

She had always loved reading, and after getting saved, she'd started reading sweet romance novels. The big-name chains carried them, of course, but she was thrilled when Notes in the Margin had put up a sign on the noticeboard at the church she attended.

She chose three more novels and headed to the counter with her treasures, stopping briefly to examine a display of journals and devotionals in the center of the foyer area.

"Good afternoon, honey. It's so good to see you again. How are you doing?" The woman sitting there was over sixty years old. She wore her hair in a short, natural style, and her glasses were a bit too big for her face. Her butterscotch skin was becoming wrinkled, and the laugh lines by her mouth told the tale of a life filled with good humor.

"I'm fine, thank you."

"You know, honey, you come in here all the time, and I've never asked your name."

"It's Claire."

"Hi, Claire. I'm Ruby Crawford, but everyone calls me Aunt Ruby."

"Nice to meet you, Aunt Ruby." Claire smiled and deposited the books on the counter. Aunt Ruby rang them up and Claire handed over her credit card and driver's license.

Aunt Ruby read the name and looked up at Claire. "You're Claire Foxwood?" She gave her a quick once-over.

She shrugged and smiled. "I am. Why do you ask?"

"You won our book giveaway last month. I was wondering who our winner was."

"I did. Thank you very much, by the way. The books were great."

"I'm sure they were."

Claire felt enveloped in Aunt Ruby's warm, welcoming smile. Now would be the perfect time to ask about Robert Marsden, but somehow, she couldn't work up the courage.

"Do you have a lot of family around here, Claire?"

"Not really. My cousin lives in St. Augustine, but my parents are in Chicago."

"What about a church family?"

"Yes, I go to one of the Episcopalian churches in town. Why do you ask?"

"My sister Emmy and I attend services at the church over on the next block. We're celebrating Friends and Fellowship Day this Sunday, and I wondered if you'd like to come by. Each of us is supposed to invite five new people."

Claire did a quick mental check to see what she would be doing this coming Sunday. It wasn't a special day at her own church, so why not? Aunt Ruby was nice enough, and a change was good every now and then. "I guess I could take a day off from my own church."

Aunt Ruby named a church Claire had passed once or twice, although she had never visited it herself.

"Service starts at eight, and we're having a potluck lunch afterward."

"That's lovely. Should I bring something?" Claire signed for her purchase and collected her credit card and license.

"You don't have to, but you're welcome to participate if you'd like."

"Great! See you Sunday." She collected her bag of books from her new friend and returned to her car. It wasn't until she was starting the engine that she realized she had forgotten about Robert Marsden for at least a few minutes. Would wonders never cease?

∽

That Saturday was particularly busy at Outside-In, and although Claire was supposed to have the afternoon off, she didn't want to leave Mitzie alone in the store. She didn't even remember about Aunt Ruby's invitation until late that evening when she was trying to figure out what to wear to church the next day.

Now that she remembered the potluck, she wanted to take something. She enjoyed cooking and baking, but she generally cooked only the things *she* liked to eat. An unrepentant pasta fiend, she could make a mean lasagna, baked ziti or mac and cheese, but she was sure there would be a wide selection of pasta dishes. She also enjoyed making a good gumbo when she had the time, but she didn't picture herself stirring a roux for the better part of an hour just to get the dish started. Since she'd had the telephone line repaired a couple days ago, she reached for the handset and called up her cousin, Jenna, who gave her an idea for an unusual baked chicken. Though it was already after eight o'clock, she headed to her favorite supermarket and picked up the ingredients: two chickens already cut into pieces, a jar of mango jam and some canned mango nectar. She'd also be making some roasted potatoes, so she picked up a large bag of potatoes and some fresh rosemary.

At home, she melted a few tablespoons of the mango jam with some of the nectar poured in. When it cooled a little, she added some to her usual homemade marinade and poured it over the chicken to marinate in the fridge overnight. She cooled the rest of the jam and nectar combination and stuck it in the fridge for basting the chicken during baking.

She also decided to save a step in the morning by peeling the potatoes and covering them with salted water so she could give them a quick boil and coat them in olive oil and rosemary before sticking them in the oven early the next morning.

She declined a last-minute invitation to the movies with a few friends and settled in with another of her new books. She didn't surface until midnight, having read every last word.

Ω

Claire groaned when the alarm clock went off at five the next morning. She hated waking up that early, but before hitting the snooze button, she remembered the potluck lunch. She said a quick prayer of thanksgiving and rolled out of bed, her eyes half-shut. Moving on auto-pilot, she put the coffee on before she did anything else. She knew her priorities, and this morning, caffeine was definitely number one. She always had the best intentions about getting to sleep early, but once she took up a book, it was the hardest thing to put it down without knowing how it ended. She always told herself, *Just one more chapter*, but even as she formed the thought, she knew she was lying to herself.

With the coffee brewing, she stuck the chicken and potatoes into the oven, set the timer, and turned on the television while settling into the recliner closest to the kitchen. Of course, she fell asleep trying to watch the televangelist, and she jumped to her feet when the oven timer went off and woke her up. After checking the chicken and potatoes, she removed them from the heat. The scent of the rosemary and roasted chicken filled the entire bungalow, and her stomach rumbled, reminding her that she hadn't even had her coffee.

She hadn't expected to fall asleep again, so now it was too late to have breakfast. What a waste of good coffee. It was already after seven o'clock when she jumped into the shower. Afterwards, she slipped on the yellow eyelet tea-length dress she'd decided on the night before. Since the dress was sleeveless and she didn't know the church's rules—written or unwritten— about modesty, she added a bright blue polished cotton jacket with three-quarter sleeves and matching peep-toe pumps. She rushed through her makeup application, taking ten minutes instead of the usual twenty. Makeup had almost become a part of her, and no matter how late she was, she always found time for a little pop of color.

ଓ

At ten minutes past eight, Claire was trotting up the stairs from the basement of Aunt Ruby's church. When she'd pulled up, someone had welcomed her and in response to her question about the potluck, had sent a muscular teenager to help her carry in the two large disposable aluminum containers. They had descended to the well-lit basement and deposited them on large trestle tables with the other dishes before heading back upstairs. There were no chairs set up, and Claire wondered where they were going to eat.

The basement stairs ended in a hallway that led to one of the side entrances of the sanctuary, so Claire slipped inside, glad she was in time to catch the start of the service. It seemed this church, like hers, used its starting time as a guideline rather than a rule.

The praise and worship session was very lively, and Claire soon found herself singing along and tapping her feet. Her church used pre-recorded worship tracks piped through speakers throughout the sanctuary, but this church boasted a live band and praise and worship team. She didn't see Aunt Ruby in the crowd of people, but she didn't feel like a stranger. All the Friends Day visitors—a group that constituted more than half of those in attendance—were welcomed by the middle-aged pastor during the service. The sermon was moving, and Claire was thrilled to see that over thirty people responded to the altar call. She would probably come back to service here. She was really enjoying it. Her mind flashed back to Robert. She wondered if she had mustered enough courage to ask Aunt Ruby about him.

CHAPTER FOUR

At the end of the service, the pastor invited everyone to join them at the park next door for the potluck lunch and then took the time to say grace before giving the benediction. Claire realized that while the service had been going on, volunteers had been moving the food to the open area next door. The park was well-equipped for events like these, with an open-sided eating area and concrete tables on the patio.

The food had been placed in the covered area, and lines formed immediately. When Claire got to the tables where the food was being served, she was pleased to finally find Aunt Ruby among a group of ladies serving plates.

There was so much food that Claire wasn't sure what to choose. She finally decided on a rich-looking chicken and seafood gumbo over rice. She added a side of buttered corn on the cob. Her mother wasn't around to frown at her, so she didn't bother with the usual charade of adding salad to her tray. Corn was a vegetable, and that had to be enough. After pouring herself a cup of lemonade, she stood wondering where to sit. There were a few empty park benches, but she didn't want to appear 'stand-offish,' as her Grandy used to say. At the same time, the people who occupied tables were already laughing and talking among themselves, and she didn't want to intrude.

Still unsure of where to go, she was pleasantly surprised when she heard her name. Aunt Ruby was approaching her with a tray in her hands. She used her chin to point to a table where an elderly woman in a wheelchair sat watching a group of children play on the swings. "Do you mind keeping my sister Emmy company? I served up this plate for her, but I can't sit with her just now. The lines are still pretty long."

Claire smiled. "No problem. Does she need help feeding herself?" She followed Aunt Ruby towards the table.

"No, no. She can handle it." They reached the table and Aunt Ruby put down the tray before moving to stand behind the wheelchair. "Emmy, this is Claire. Claire, meet my sister, Emerald Donahue."

Claire reached for the wrinkled hand and shook it warmly as the woman's face broke into a smile. Up close, she wasn't as old as Claire had thought she was. She doubted that the woman had even reached seventy. Such a pity she was already wheelchair-bound.

"Claire, how nice to meet you. Come sit by me and tell me all about yourself."

Claire put her tray down and sat close to the end of the park table-bench combination where the wheelchair had been parked. "Well, Ms. Donahue—" she began, but was cut off immediately.

"Please, call me Aunt Emmy. Everyone else does."

Claire grinned. She liked these two women. "Well, Aunt Emmy, I'm Claire Foxwood and I—"

She was cut off again, "Claire Foxwood... Claire Foxwood... are you related to Reverend Charles Foxwood of the AME Church?"

"No, ma'am. My folks are in Chicago. Except for my cousin, Jenna. She married a man from St. Augustine and when she told me about the sunny winters, I followed her here."

"I see. And how old are you?"

"I'm twenty-eight, ma'am. How old are you?" Claire grinned to show that she was only being facetious.

"I'm younger than I feel and older than I look, my dear." Aunt Emmy's smile was genuine.

"Good answer." Claire noticed that Aunt Ruby had disappeared. Claire didn't mind. She enjoyed spending time with older folks, and it wasn't like Aunt Emmy was an invalid or lost in her own world; on the contrary, she was quite alert.

"Anyway, you were saying something about your work."

"Oh, yes. I'm a makeup artist."

"How lovely, dear. The world has just about enough doctors and lawyers, if you ask me."

A few tables away, a toddler got away from her mother, who was trying to feed a child who looked like the runaway's twin. Claire was able to grab the child as she ran past. Laughing, she took her back to her mother, who smiled gratefully as Claire headed back to her table.

"That was nice of you. Are you a lover of children, my dear?"

"I am, ma'am."

"Nice. Do you have any of your own?"

"No, ma'am. I've never been married."

Aunt Emmy drew her eyes to Claire's. "I must admit it's nice to hear that from a young woman such as yourself. It seems that young people's priorities are quite different now than when I was a girl in my twenties."

Claire grinned. It had been a long time since anyone had referred to her as a girl.

"Why haven't you married?"

It seemed Aunt Emmy didn't believe in wasting time. Claire chewed her gumbo thoughtfully before responding. "I don't want to sound cliché, but I guess I haven't found the right person just yet."

"And how hard have you tried, dear?" Aunt Emmy watched her over the rim of her glass.

Claire almost choked on her food. She cleared her throat and reached for her lemonade. When she recovered, she chuckled. "Not that hard, I have to admit. Getting married is not a high priority for me right now."

"Well, what is?" Aunt Emmy was clearly enjoying the lasagna Aunt Ruby had served for her. Unlike Claire, her plate was loaded with a salad comprised of crispy lettuce, juicy tomatoes, and what appeared to be walnuts and grapes. For a fleeting second, Claire wondered if she should go get some salad, then she caught herself. Had her mind been taken over by salad-loving pod people for just a moment? Crazy! She struggled to remember what Aunt Emmy had asked her.

"My priorities? I guess I'm building my business and I'm trying to figure out God's purpose for my life. Until I do that, I can't walk in it."

Even as Aunt Emmy spoke, Claire noticed that she was looking over Claire's shoulder at someone in the background. Claire resisted the urge to turn around. Aunt Emmy found Claire's eyes and looked at her knowingly. "That's reasonable, I suppose. Unless His purpose for your life is tied to your future husband's purpose. And if that's the case, how will you ever meet the man if all you're doing is working and praying, and praying and working?"

Claire's fork fell. As she bent to retrieve it, an image of Robert Marsden appeared in her mind's eye. It was so unexpected that she found herself shaken.

She barely had time to recover before she noticed Aunt Emmy waving at someone behind her. "Come over here, sweetheart, and join us."

As soon as Claire turned around, her mouth fell open.

☙

Robert Marsden had been having a challenging day, to say the very least. Early that morning, after spending the night on the lumpy sofa at a friend's apartment following a marathon study session, he had been on his way from the seminary when his car had fallen into a pothole, and he had ended up with not one, but *two* flat tires. Of course, he only had one spare, so he had replaced the one that looked worse off and had driven at a snail's pace until he got to a gas station. It turned out the other tire was too worn to be fixed properly, so he had ended up having to buy two new ones he hadn't budgeted for this month. By the time he had hit the Jacksonville city limits, he was so tired, dirty and annoyed that he had gone straight to his apartment and cleaned up.

He'd needed a moment to rest his eyes, and by the time he woke up, he had already missed most of the service at church. Robert had pulled himself out of bed and sat on the edge with his head in his hands. He was tired. So very tired. It seemed he always was.

Disgusted with himself for falling asleep, he'd almost decided to stay home for the day, but it was after midday, and he was yet to even think about Sunday dinner. He'd decided to go to the church potluck after all.

As soon as he'd arrived at the park, Robert had headed straight for the lunch line. Aunt Ruby, who helped him out by working in the bookstore several afternoons a week, had loaded his plate with more chicken, roast beef, dinner rolls, potatoes and lasagna than one person should eat in one sitting.

"I see you're running yourself ragged again," she had chastised.

Robert had offered a wry smile, knowing she was right.

"I guess a free hot meal is what it'll take to pull you away from all the running around." She'd winked to show him she wasn't being too serious while she added a second plate full of salad. He protested that he couldn't eat that much, but she only smiled at him and pointed him in the direction of her sister, Aunt Emmy.

As Aunt Emmy made eye contact with him, she beckoned him over. "Come over here, sweetheart, and join us."

He wasn't sure who was sitting beside her, since the woman's back was to him, but he caught the curve of her face as she bent to retrieve something. The woman sat up and turned around; he couldn't help but notice the shock that had registered on her beautiful countenance.

He gave a quick look behind him to see if there was someone there, but there wasn't. She obviously recognized him, but Robert had absolutely no idea who she was.

He gave Aunt Emmy the obligatory kiss on the cheek before placing his tray across the table from them. He greeted them both as he sat.

"I missed you at service this morning." Aunt Emmy looked at him in mock disapproval. "Ruby had to push my wheelchair in."

Her unasked question was rewarded with an explanation of his absence. "I have a presentation bright and early Monday evening, so I was going over everything with the rest of the group. I stayed over last night—on Roger's sofa, as usual—and had every intention of getting here in time for service. Alas! It wasn't meant to be. Two flat tires did away with that plan."

"Oh, no! I'm sorry to hear that, son. You missed a great sermon. At least a couple dozen people went to the altar, too, praise the Lord! Anyway, at least you're here now. And in one piece, I might add."

He smiled. The stranger was looking everywhere except at him. She looked vaguely familiar, but he couldn't quite remember where he may have seen her before. Maybe he had seen her in the store. But he doubted that. He would have remembered those high cheekbones. He looked at her with expectation.

"Robert Marsden, do you know Claire..." Aunt Emmy turned to Claire and asked, "I'm sorry. What did you say your last name was, honey?"

"Foxwood."

"Ah, yes. But no relation to Reverend Foxwood." Aunt Emmy remembered what she'd been saying and repeated the question. "Do you know Claire Foxwood, honey?"

Claire Foxwood. The name sounded vaguely familiar, but he still couldn't place her.

Just as he was about to shake his head in response to Aunt Emmy's question, Claire answered. "We've met." She looked uncomfortable.

"We have?" Robert asked, his brow wrinkled. He put down the dinner roll he had been about to devour.

"Yes."

"Are you sure?"

"I'm sure."

"Where?"

She smiled mysteriously. "Maybe it will come to you."

So, she's going to keep me guessing, huh? Robert thought to himself. "Suit yourself," he shrugged.

Her smile didn't quite reach her eyes, causing him to get the impression she was upset with him, he had to admit that she was beautiful. That gap between her two front teeth was a bit wide for his liking, but it did nothing to detract from her beauty. Her makeup was impeccably applied, and though he wasn't a fan of what he liked to call 'war paint,' he couldn't really find any flaws with it. It was so understated that the only reason he really knew she was wearing makeup was the fact that her complexion was more flawless than any human being's skin had a right to be. The word *dewy* came to mind, but he couldn't figure out how to use it in a sentence, even if it was only in his mind.

He bit into the roll hungrily. He hadn't eaten all day. He had hoped to bring something to the potluck, but he knew there would have been enough for everyone; they wouldn't miss his one or two dishes. He used his knife and fork to cut off a sliver of the chicken breast. He was a dark meat man, usually, but one of the consequences of turning up late was that all the drumsticks and thighs had already been taken. He hoped the meat wouldn't be too dry.

"Mmm." He couldn't help but voice his pleasure when the breast turned out to be perfectly moist. Another bite proved that it was seasoned all the way through.

"Good?" Aunt Emmy had finished eating and was watching him with pleasure.

"Awesomely good. Did Aunt Ruby make it?" He cut off a bigger bite this time and added some of the roasted potatoes to his fork.

Aunt Emmy shook her head. "No. She made the roast beef and a tuna casserole."

He took her hint and speared some of the succulent beef. It was heavenly, but he had expected that. Aunt Ruby had once told him that she let the roast marinate in the fridge for two days if she could.

"The roast is perfect, as usual, Aunt Emmy. My regards to the chef. To be honest, I'm not usually a fan of baked chicken, but this is good. Did you taste it?" He looked at both women. "It has a hint of something… it's sweet but savory at the same time. Kind of fruity… I'm not sure."

"Actually, I think that's the chicken I brought," the enigmatic Claire Foxwood claimed.

He chewed thoughtfully and swallowed before taking a swig of cola. "*You* brought this?"

"I did. Why would I say I brought it if I didn't?" Her tone was more than a tad offensive, and Robert held his hands up in his own defense. "I used mango jam and nectar."

"No need to get defensive, Mrs. Foxwood." He wondered if she knew he was fishing for information. She wasn't wearing a wedding band, but that meant little these days.

"It's *Miss* Foxwood, actually, but feel free to call me Claire."

"Well, Claire," Aunt Emmy began, "it takes quite a lot to impress this man when it comes to good food. He's quite the chef himself, you know."

"I see."

Robert wondered what he had said or done to make this pretty woman so clearly upset. Was it because he didn't remember her? In his work at the bookstore and his studies at the college, he came into contact with a lot of different people on a daily basis. He couldn't help it if he was bad with both names *and* faces. He shook his head as he turned his full attention to the plate, determined to keep quiet for the rest of the meal. The chicken was pretty good, though, and now that she had said it, he could identify a hint of mango flavor throughout. He wondered if he could replicate it. He'd ask for the recipe, but she might bite his head off. He shook his head again. *Women!*

 લ

Claire couldn't help it. When she was uncomfortable, she became defensive, and to overcompensate for the defensiveness, she usually went on the offensive. Without even intending to, she'd done the same thing with Robert Marsden. What was it Saint Paul had said? The things he wanted to do he didn't do, but the things he didn't want to do… *those* were the things he did. And he was a saint!

She was sure her heart had skipped two or three beats—maybe even thirty—when he'd strolled into her line of vision. Again, she had felt a very strong sensation that this man would have some kind of significant impact on her life, but she couldn't tell whether she would appreciate or rue it.

What she *could* tell in that moment was that she found him extremely attractive. And she could see she wasn't the only one. All around the park, women of all ages were practically salivating as they sent furtive glances in his direction, and several were shooting darts at Claire, she guessed because she was the one sitting at the same table. If only they knew. She'd rather be anywhere else.

It wasn't that she didn't know she was treating him unfairly. She knew it, and she didn't want to, but it seemed that whenever she felt cornered, she felt she had no choice but to lash out. The sad thing was, Robert Marsden didn't have a clue about the kind of effect his mere presence was having on her, so she knew he was probably wondering why she was acting the way she was. She just couldn't help it. Why couldn't she have accepted the indirect compliment when he had spoken so highly of the dish she had prepared? Why did she have to go all verbal Tae Kwan Do on him? No wonder he had clammed up. She would have, too.

She said a quick prayer for guidance and turned to look at Aunt Emmy, who was looking at her with an impish smile on her face.

The older woman smiled at her, "There are many great things about Robert here, Claire; he has a number of skills and talents, but I know for sure that the ability to place a face and a name is not one of them. If I were a gambling woman, I'd bet my last dime that he has no idea where you've met before, but he's too much of a man to ask again." Claire noticed that Robert was staring at Aunt Emmy with an expression of disbelief on his handsome face.

She had a quick internal debate about whether or not to respond, but Aunt Emmy was obviously trying to ease the palpable tension around the table, so she complied. "A few weeks ago, my name was drawn in a contest at the Notes in the Margin bookstore, which is where I met Aunt Ruby. He delivered the prize to my house. Maybe he remembers my German Shepherd, Chaz."

Claire couldn't help but notice the shock on Robert's face while she was speaking. He furrowed his brow.

"You *do* remember Chaz, don't you?" Claire prompted him.

"I remember going to a house and leaving a box on the door mat. I remember a yapping dog behind a screen door. But I certainly don't remember you. I'm sure if—" he swallowed the rest of whatever he was going to say.

Claire shrugged as if it were no big deal, but she couldn't decide if she was happy or sad that she had been so *forgettable*, even though he had never been far from her thoughts for more than an hour or two since their first encounter.

Robert took another bite of chicken and chewed thoughtfully as if he was thinking hard. Claire watched as the gap in his memory was suddenly bridged, and he finally figured it out.

"Aww, man! Not Big B—?" He snapped his mouth shut again, but his eyes had registered some kind of recognition.

Claire frowned. It would have been better if he *hadn't* remembered. Again, she went on the offensive, afraid that she would never get over his next words if she allowed him to speak first. "I see you remember. I must have been quite a sight in my big yellow robe. You caught me at a bad time... halfway through my bath."

"I'm sorry." He seemed genuinely surprised. He tried unsuccessfully to swallow a chuckle, which resulted in a coughing fit and a little sputtering. He ducked his head, but Claire could see by the tilt of his face that he was surreptitiously trying to survey her even as he tried to clear his throat. Her flesh rose up and she stood with her tray. She needed a moment.

"Excuse me while I go get some dessert. May I get anything for either of you?" Even as she spoke, she noticed he was doing a good job of looking into her eyes rather than at her figure. She was glad she had chosen the yellow dress. It hugged her waist and flared at the hips before falling in folds to just below her knees.

"Nothing for me, please. I'm so full I couldn't even take a message right now!" Aunt Emmy smiled.

"Any kind of sweet treat, please. I'm partial to sweetness…" Claire could tell that Robert's pause was deliberate, "… in things like cake and such. Thank you."

She tried not to swing her hips as she walked away, but it was hard not to put on a show for his benefit. At first, she had been annoyed that he had forgotten her, then she'd found herself even more annoyed when he had remembered exactly how she had looked that day. She didn't even know what she wanted!

She held her head up as she measured her steps toward the dessert table. This attractive man who'd made such an impression on her had seen her at her worst. She wanted him to remember what she looked like at her best. She knew that if he was like most single men she knew, his eyes would be glued to her ample hips as she walked away. She added a little extra sashay to her walk as she made her way to the dessert table. Searing her image on his retina the way his had been etched into hers was going to be easier than she thought.

CHAPTER FIVE

By the time he heard Aunt Emmy clearing her throat, Robert suspected she had been doing just that for some time. He looked over at her, and when she started chuckling in that way that only she could, he knew he'd been busted. He smiled sheepishly.

"Do you mind telling me what that was all about?" she asked with a grin.

Robert explained the circumstances under which they had met and tried to describe the woman he remembered seeing. "I've got to be honest with you, Aunt Emmy, I'm still not sure it was her. I mean, this person came to the door and with those oversized glasses, I couldn't tell if she was a teenager or someone as—shall we say, mature?—as you. No offense, Aunt Emmy."

She shrugged. "None taken. Go on." She hurried him along with her hand.

He waved his hands in the air as he tried to find the right words to describe the spectacle he'd seen. "She was just so... yellow. And orange. With a polka-dotted shower cap. And the dog kept barking for a while. I didn't pay too much attention. I just did what I went to do and left."

"I see. And just now, when you were watching her walk away?"

Robert looked down at his plate to hide his blush. "Well... I may be a Christian and future pastor, Aunt Emmy, but I'm still a man."

She nodded with understanding. "Now I understand why she was so annoyed with you earlier."

"Annoyed?"

"Yes. Clearly, she remembered you from your first meeting, but you didn't remember her. And now that you do… well, I guess we always want other people's first impression of us to be good. Not laughable."

"Yeah, I can see how that would get her goat. But it's not my fault, Aunt Emmy. Look at her today. What you see over there is a woman who spent a lot of time getting dressed this morning. Look at her hair, her makeup. I'm surprised she didn't whip her compact out right at the table to ensure that she was still perfect."

"Hmmm. I actually think she looks quite nice. And I find her makeup to be minimal."

"I think that's the impression she wants to give. I think she's one of those women who spends a lot of time trying to look like that's how she wakes up in the morning. And look how upset she seems to be over the fact that I forgot her. Like she's not used to that happening and she wants me to regret it."

Aunt Emmy tapped her index finger to her lips like she always did when she was deep in thought. "You know something, Robert? I think you're reading this whole situation — and Miss Foxwood — all wrong, but I suppose time will tell. Now hurry up and eat your food; here comes your dessert."

Robert looked up in time to see Claire walking back to the table with a tray in her hands, the swell of her breasts hovering over red velvet cake, cheese pastries and glazed donuts. *Delicious,* he thought. She placed the tray in the middle of the table and sat down again. He looked at all the other items on the tray and raised his eyebrows at Claire in an unvoiced question.

"You said you liked… sweets." She took the cover off her cup and blew some of the steam away before putting it to her lips.

"Are you trying to fatten me up, woman?" Robert was serious, so he was quite surprised when she started to laugh.

Her chuckles were contagious, and before long, he found himself laughing along with her.

Robert wasn't sure whether it was the simple act of service despite being upset with him, or the sound of her laughter, but without warning, he found his curiosity piqued. The laughter had eased the tension somewhat, and it was only now that he was relaxing that he realized how wound up he had been since their conversation had begun.

ര

In bed that night, Claire found herself reflecting on a number of unanswered questions about Robert Marsden. She supposed her insatiable curiosity had something to do with the number of mystery novels she was always reading, but she couldn't figure out which had come first—the curiosity or the love of cozy mysteries.

They had parted on fairly amicable terms after the somewhat rocky start to their reintroduction. Aunt Ruby had joined them after a while, and she and her sister had entertained them with stories of their childhood with their siblings, Sapphire and Garnet. Their mother, they explained, had grown up in poverty and had found comfort telling herself that someday she would be surrounded by precious stones. When her children had come along, she had named each of them after a different gem so she'd have a constant reminder that they were all the riches she needed in life. It was an endearing tale for Claire, but she could see that Robert found it too ridiculous for words. Even as she listened to the older women spinning tales, she couldn't stop herself from wondering what made this man tick.

She couldn't deny that she'd love to find out more about him, but she had no idea when or even *if* she would see him again. She'd never found out the relationship between Robert and Notes in the Margin. Maybe Aunt Ruby owned the store and had just asked him to deliver the box because he lived in the neighborhood. All she had been able to deduce was that he was a student and a member of Aunt Ruby's church. Her curiosity was at an all-time high, so she actually had to promise herself that she wouldn't start visiting their church more often *just* so she could see this man again. That would never do. As she had told Aunt Emmy, she needed to figure out what the Lord wanted her to do moving forward and concentrate her efforts there.

As soon as the thought had formed in her mind, she remembered what Aunt Emmy had said to her just before Robert had made his appearance that day. Something about the possibility that her own purpose was tied in to that of her future husband. She wondered what had inspired Aunt Emmy to make that cryptic statement while staring at Robert Marsden. Again, Claire couldn't shake the feeling that her destiny was somehow inextricably linked to this man. She whispered a word of prayer, asking the Lord to show her His plans for her life and to open and close the right doors so that she would end up exactly where He wanted her.

She had, in a way, been praying about her future husband for a long time, just as her parents had implored her to do. Even so, she wasn't yearning for marriage the way her favorite cousin and best friend, Jenna, had done. She was happy living her life just the way she wanted—going where she wanted to go, doing what she wanted to do, consulting only God for guidance.

She had read the scripture that spoke about a wife submitting to her husband, and her prayers were for the Lord to send her a man she'd be comfortable submitting to. She didn't relish the idea. She envisioned marriage as a surrendering of her life and her dreams—abstract though they were—in favor of her family's, and she was willing to delay that for a number of years. She was still young; there was still time. Ideally, she wouldn't marry before thirty, and the children wouldn't come for another few years after that. She wanted time to get to know her husband before bringing children into the home. She expected to be a very involved wife and mother, and she just knew that her time would be fully consumed by those who depended on her. Until then, she had a business to run and personal goals to accomplish. She would stick to the plan no matter what.

CB

Robert was beyond tired. As he lay in bed that Sunday night, the weeks and months and years stretched ahead of him, and he wondered when he would be able to get some *real* rest. He sighed. Hadn't the Lord Jesus Himself said those who were weary should come to Him, and He would give them rest? Yet it was only after he had decided to go to seminary that Robert had begun to feel this exhausted. As he waited for sleep to visit him for a few hours, he couldn't stop himself from looking back on his life over the past year or two.

He had become a Christian in his mid-twenties, after he'd gotten a degree in business and had begun working at a major bookstore chain. He'd moved through the ranks until he was named assistant manager. After a couple of years learning more about management than a degree had ever taught him, he'd decided to open his own bookstore—a much smaller, more family-friendly operation that he'd be able to manage himself. He wanted to know his customers by name and to be able to choose books that would be encouraging, uplifting or entertaining, and preferably a combination of all of the above. His dream was to be able to open a shipment of assorted used books and call up a particular customer to tell them that he had just found the perfect book for them. It had taken some time, but Notes in the Margin was finally in the black, and he had a steady stream of customers visiting, many on a weekly basis.

And then he had gotten what he liked to refer to as *The Call*. While sitting in Bible study one Wednesday evening, he'd listened as the pastor had expounded on a scripture from the second chapter of Second Timothy. "Study to show yourself approved unto God, a workman that needs not to be ashamed, rightly dividing the word of truth." Robert had felt the firm grip of a hand on his right shoulder. Almost as soon as he felt it, the hand moved. He was sitting at the end of the row, so he turned around, but the only people who were sitting there were a couple of middle-aged women. Surely neither of them had such a strong grip!

Worried he might have imagined it, he'd turned back to the discussion at hand, and once again, he'd had the same sensation. There was no mistake about it—there was definitely a man's hand on his shoulder. Again, he had turned, and again there had been no one there. He'd understood that he was receiving some kind of holy visitation. Closing his eyes, he had bowed his head and begun to pray for the Lord to speak to him. Though there had been no audible words, he'd somehow known that the Lord, through this invisible messenger whose hand he could still feel, was telling him that He had chosen him to be a minister of the Word. As sure as he was sitting there praying, he'd known he was being called to preach. Preaching had never entered his mind before that night, but afterward, he'd found himself rather hard-pressed to get it out of his thoughts.

Despite the visitation, he still hadn't been sure about becoming a minister, so he'd prayed about it, read the Bible and prayed some more. He hadn't discussed the leading with anyone, but a week later, on his way to Bible study, he had prayed that the Lord would confirm His instruction through someone he had never spoken to before.

"Lord, if this is really You," he'd prayed silently, afraid the devil would hear his petition and use his own words against him, "please use someone at church to confirm it. I want to be used by You in any way You see fit, and if becoming a minister is what You would have me do, please allow a stranger to ask me if I ever considered becoming a pastor. I thank You, Lord, that even in the silence of this vehicle, You hear my prayer and will give me a clear answer tonight. I pray in Jesus' name, amen."

As soon as he'd parked his car and stepped into the sanctuary, he'd been greeted by the two gray-haired sisters who always sat behind him. They had been standing just inside the sanctuary door, one leaning heavily on a cane and the other standing next to her.

"Hello, young man," the one with the cane had greeted him. "I'm Emmy Donahue and this is my baby sister, Ruby Crawford." The so-called 'baby' sister could probably be Robert's mother, but he'd nodded his head in greeting.

"My name is Robert Marsden."

"Marsden… Marsden… are you related to Bishop Marsden of the Church of God in Christ over near Jacksonville Beach?" She'd moved towards him slowly, as if testing the strength of the cane, and peered into his face.

"Not that I'm aware of, ma'am. I don't have any bishops in my family."

"Pity, pity," she'd continued.

"Why's that, ma'am?"

"You look like you could be a preacher. Isn't that right, Ruby?" She had turned to look at her 'baby' sister.

"I suppose so, Emmy, but he also looks like he could be a teacher or a doctor or a salesman. I mean, what does a preacher even look like?" Unlike the elder of the two, Mrs. Crawford wore her hair very short.

"Like him." Mrs. Donahue had turned her face towards his again. "Have you ever thought about being a pastor, son?"

Robert had found himself swallowing hard. That was fast. "Not until around a week ago, ma'am," he'd confirmed.

"Well, don't hesitate, son. The Word of God tells us that the harvest is plentiful, but the laborers are few. Says so right there in Luke chapter ten and two."

"Yes, ma'am. May I help you to your usual seat?"

Emmy had smiled. "See there? Now, that's something a pastor would do. We were waiting on you, you know?"

Robert had wrinkled his brow. "You were? Why?" He was horrible with names and faces, but he was positive he'd never spoken to either of them before.

"The temperature in there is too low, son. What did you say your name was? I'm not as old as I look, but I must admit I was so distracted by your handsome face that I forgot."

"His name is Robert Marsden, Emmy. Don't you remember? You practically accused him of being Bishop Marsden's illegitimate son," Mrs. Crawford had exaggerated.

"Tut, tut, Ruby," Mrs. Donahue had clucked. "Don't get annoyed with me. You know I've never been good with names." She'd looked at Robert again. "Robert, we were waiting on you because so few young men come to Bible study, but you're always here. Always, always. I said to Ruby, 'Let's just wait on that handsome young man who always sits right in front of us.' Isn't that what I said, Ruby? I just knew you could somehow adjust the air conditioning. When it's too cold in there, my old bones act up, and I have enough aches and pains without that."

"No problem, ma'am. I'll see what I can do."

"Please, call her Aunt Emmy. Everybody does." The younger of the two said. "And I'm Aunt Ruby. We know we're old, but we don't like to be reminded with this 'ma'am, ma'am' business everywhere we turn."

"Pleased to meet you both. My mother is the same way." He smiled as he headed to adjust the thermostat. It actually *was* frigid in the sanctuary. He'd shaken his head as he walked. "Okay, God, I hear You. Ministry it is."

That had been two years ago. It had taken him a year to put aside enough money to register for a degree in ministry at a seminary in Jacksonville. It was the closest one to his home, but it was still over half an hour away. He had scheduled most of his classes for evenings, after the bookstore closed at six, but there had been a couple day classes he'd had to attend. Since he couldn't afford full-time staff at the bookstore—not if he wanted to keep all his bills covered—he'd considered delaying school for another year, but Aunt Ruby and Aunt Emmy wouldn't hear of it.

In the ensuing time, Aunt Emmy's medical condition—he always forgot its name, but it had something to do with her back—had deteriorated to the point that sometimes she needed a wheelchair; even so, she had insisted that Aunt Ruby help out in the store a few hours per week in order for Robert to go to classes. A lover of reading, Aunt Ruby hadn't needed much convincing.

Aunt Emmy wasn't an invalid. There were times she could move around well enough with her cane, but when her back started to act up, she would use the wheelchair. Fiercely independent, she still lived alone despite her son Daniel's desire for the two sisters to move in together. In Aunt Emmy's words, "The only thing worse than an old biddy is two old biddies living together!" Robert and Aunt Ruby had agreed that if an emergency should arise while he was at school, she should do what she needed to do, even if it meant closing the store in the middle of the day.

Robert could see that God had provided a way for him to *study and show himself approved* while managing his business and staying out of too much debt.

He just wished he could do it all without being so, so *tired* all the time. He felt as if he was on one continuous cycle of going to work, going to classes, studying and going to church. There were times he had slept through the alarm clock and had actually opened the store late. He knew he probably couldn't keep this up for the remaining three semesters in his current program, but he was determined to do what he could and trust God to do the rest.

As he pounded his pillow into the perfect shape, he reminded himself that it was a good thing he wasn't married or involved with anyone, because he would never be able to find the time for a family. He'd had several girlfriends, of course, but there was no one he could imagine spending the rest of his life with. He wasn't really looking, but he'd begun to wonder if such a woman even existed. He had barely completed the thought when, for some inexplicable reason, Claire Foxwood's image appeared in his mind's eye. *Stop it,* he scolded himself. *She's not even my type.*

CHAPTER SIX

To say that Claire Foxwood wasn't a fan of exercise was to make the understatement of the century. The very *thought* of doing anything more physically demanding than lifting bottles of foundation or a stack of books was enough to have her breaking a sweat. At the same time, she knew her beloved pet needed to stretch his legs now and then. She tried to take him for a walk at least once every two or three days, even though he spent a couple of hours in the yard every evening after she got home. More often than not, the walk would turn into a run as she tried — and failed — to contain his boundless enthusiasm.

A few Saturdays after chatting with Aunt Ruby at the bookstore, Claire came home from Outside-In to find Chaz in an energetic mood. Before she could convince herself not to, she changed into black sweatpants with a matching top and sneakers and grabbed the leash from its place near the front door. The moment she got the leash, the German Shepherd became even more animated, and his excitement was contagious. Although Claire would rather be reading, she couldn't help but smile at the dog's antics.

They headed to the end of the walkway, the dog leading the owner, as was always the case. This time, instead of turning left like he usually did, Chaz flipped the script by turning right. Claire complied. They had only been walking for a couple of minutes when Claire had to pull back hard on the leash to prevent the dog from running in front of a car that was turning out of the parking lot of a two-story apartment complex. The driver slammed on his brakes before making a rude hand gesture and gunning the car. Claire bent to make sure her dog was okay, and on hearing another vehicle turning into the parking lot, she shortened the length of the leash and stood.

The driver of the dark-colored sedan turning into the parking lot was none other than Robert Marsden. She waited on the sidewalk as he pulled into the first available spot, and as he stepped out of the car, Chaz began to strain against the leash. It was clear that he wanted to go check out the car. Claire hesitated for a moment, but when Robert smiled and waved, she ignored her better judgment and headed in his direction.

"Hey, Robert," she greeted him.

He surprised her by remembering her name. "Claire, it's good to see you. Where are you two headed?" Robert tilted his head in the direction of the dog, who was busy marking his territory on the car's front bumper. Claire considered reprimanding him, but he went to investigate something in the nearby grass, so she didn't bother. He was a well-behaved, friendly dog, but she kept a firm grip on his leash nevertheless.

"We're just taking a walk."

He eyed her from head to toe and she almost squirmed under his gaze. She looked down at her outfit and wondered if he could tell that she almost never wore it. Why would she? She almost never exercised.

"Nice dog. Quiet."

She smiled. "Yeah, he only gets defensive on home ground. Is this where you live?" She waved towards the apartment building behind him.

"Well, it's where I sleep."

It was her turn to raise an eyebrow. In response to her unvoiced question, Robert elaborated. "I'm pretty busy with the store and school, so I basically come home to sleep."

"The bookstore?" Maybe he worked there part-time.

"Yeah. I'm there most of the week, but Aunt Ruby fills in when I have classes."

Aha. Now she understood.

"So it's yours?"

"That's what it says on the lease. Why?"

"No reason. I like the hometown feel of it. It's a lot more personal than the chain stores. And I love the selection."

"Thanks. That's exactly what I was going for." He smiled.

"And you're in school?" she asked.

"Yeah. Seminary."

"Really? Studying to become a preacher, are you?"

"Yep."

"Good luck with that." She couldn't see him as a preacher, but she didn't want to tell him that. Not wanting her disbelief to show, she smiled brightly.

"Thanks. Actually, I'm supposed to be leading a Bible study as part of my field work. It will be at the seminary on Monday night. It's open to the public. I already invited Aunt Ruby and Aunt Emmy, but I won't be able to take them since I have classes that afternoon. You have a car, right?"

"Yeah." Anticipating where he was going, she continued. "I could take them, no problem."

"Thanks so much. Aunt Emmy's wheelchair is collapsible, so if she needs it you can just stick it in the trunk."

"Okay."

"If you give me your cell phone number, I'll text you the details."

Claire thought for second, *It's time to stir things up.* "If you want my number, Mr. Marsden, just ask." She smiled and looked towards her shoes in a move she knew highlighted her perfectly mascaraed lashes.

"Um… no… I only… um…."

What? The articulate Mr. Marsden? Rendered speechless? Claire began to smile, but changed her mind halfway when she heard, "No. I only need to send you the address. I won't call you or anything."

"Such a shame," she said before she could stop herself.

He began to look uncomfortable, so she tugged on the leash and the dog came to sit at her heel. "Well, I think Chaz is ready to go, so let me give you my number and we'll be on our way." She supplied the information, which he captured with his phone and waved goodbye.

"Take care. See you Monday."

Claire felt quite self-conscious as she turned and allowed Chaz to lead her back to the street, but when she turned to see if she and her child-bearing hips were attracting any attention, all she saw was Robert opening the door to a ground-floor apartment and heading indoors. Strange. Today, it seemed like she had no effect on him at all. If she didn't know he went to Aunt Ruby's church, she'd have wondered if he was training to become a *monk*. She followed Chaz all the way around the block, glad they could avoid the apartment complex on their way home. She had no idea how she felt about seeing Robert on Monday.

☙

On the evening of the Bible study, Claire picked up Aunt Ruby at the bookstore at a few minutes past six then followed the older woman's directions to pick up Aunt Emmy. She listened with great amusement as the two older women argued over which of them looked more like their beloved mother. By the time they turned into the long driveway of the seminary, Claire felt more relaxed than she had thought possible, considering she was about to see the man that was interfering with her dreams even though she'd been trying hard not to think about him when she was awake.

She'd been stunned when he had said he only wanted her number to text the information to her, and in the two days since she had given it to him, that's all he'd done. Her pride had taken a small hit, and she was disappointed that he didn't seem interested, but she had swallowed whatever pride she had left and decided to attend the Bible study. Aunt Ruby and Aunt Emmy were depending on her to get them to the seminary. Besides, she was quite curious herself.

This would be her first Bible study in the eleven months or so since she'd gone to the altar on a visit to the church closest to her house. She spent some time in devotion every morning, and she went to church, but that was it. She treasured her Wednesdays, and she had her routine down pat: work, home, bath, book, bed. Her devotional guide included scriptures and she read that six days a week, so in a way, she *was* studying the Bible, wasn't she?

Robert's directions had been precise, and Claire turned into the long driveway of the seminary a few minutes before seven o'clock. The campus was small by modern standards, but Claire liked the green lawns, the many shade trees and the white-trimmed brick buildings. Still, she didn't envy the students she saw walking up the steps of what appeared to be the library. She was naturally academically inclined, but she hated studying.

She identified the building Robert had described and dropped Aunt Emmy and Aunt Ruby close to the door before making her way to the parking lot.

They found the lecture theater without any challenges and soon, Claire and her two new 'aunts' were seated inside. As she waited for the session to begin, she took a look around the lecture theater. The floor sloped toward the front of the room, where there was a stage with a lectern and a desk behind it. There were spotlights directed towards the stage, leaving the rest of the room only partially lit. A few people milled around.

Some appeared to be students while others looked more like faculty, but it was hard to miss the fact that less than half the available seats were filled.

From their spot close to the entrance at the back of the lecture theater, Claire noticed Robert sitting in the very front row with his head bowed in what appeared to be prayer; several books were spread across his lap.

At precisely seven o'clock, an older gentleman approached the microphone on the stage and introduced Robert as the student whose turn it was to lead Bible study that week as part of his field work. He extended an open invitation to the audience to return every Monday for the next few weeks to hear the remaining students deliver their material.

Robert took the stage with confidence, and when he smiled, Claire's breathing grew shallow with excitement. There it was again—that sense of certainty that her destiny was somehow entwined with his. How was it that he didn't feel it, too? Even in extending the invitation to the Bible study, he hadn't been warm and welcoming, despite his smile. It was as if it was something he *had* to do, rather than something he actually *wanted* to do. She looked around the room and wondered if he had some kind of quota he'd been trying to fill—a particular number of attendees that would give him a better chance at a higher grade for the activity. It didn't look like he'd done a good job of that; there were way too many empty seats in the small lecture theater.

She wondered if he could see her in the audience, but with the lights trained on him, she knew he probably couldn't. The room was a bit too cool for Aunt Emmy's liking, so they had sat in the very last row where the air conditioning unit would blow the cold air over their heads instead of directly onto them. It was dark, and Robert probably didn't even notice that there were three people sitting back there.

Claire tried to zone in on what he was saying. She had brought her Bible and a fresh notebook with her, so she reached for her pen and opened the spiral-bound book. The projector advised that the scriptures to be studied were First Peter 3:1-12 and First Timothy 2:8-10, so she turned to the first one she found and had just started reading it when Robert's greeting brought her attention back to the stage. She slipped her finger between the pages to mark her spot.

"Good evening, everyone."

The audience murmured in response, and Robert smiled at them. "I'm sure you can do a little better than that. Good evening!" He spoke a little louder this time.

"Good evening!" Claire's voice was perhaps the loudest in the room, and she half-expected everyone to turn and stare at her. No one did.

"As Dr. Crouch mentioned, this Bible study is part of my field work, but more than that, it's an opportunity for me to share my understanding of some scripture with you. Up until a couple of days ago, I wasn't sure what I wanted to focus on, but then I had an encounter with someone, and as soon as it was over, the topic for tonight's discussion was clear.

"Imagine you're a relatively young Christian man focused on his walk with the Lord and fulfilling his God-given purpose in life. Imagine you've made a decision that with all that's going on in your life right now—school and church and owning your own business and more—you're not going to allow yourself to be distracted by a romantic relationship at this point. Imagine you know, like the great Saint Paul himself, that romance can distract people from dedicating themselves fully to the Lord's work. Are you with me so far?"

A few people in the rows in front of Claire—mainly students, she noticed—voiced their agreement.

"Great. Now imagine you are approached by a young woman—a *church-goer* you met recently through mutual friends—and despite the fact that you show absolutely no interest in her, she begins flirting with you as soon as she learns you have intentions of becoming a pastor.

"Up until now, she's barely even smiled in your direction, but suddenly, she's all smiles and fluttering eyelashes. It was clear to me that my future in the pulpit led her to have immediate aspirations of becoming the revered first lady of some mega church."

Claire sat up in her seat. Had he just said, "It was *Claire*"? She settled down again when she figured out that he had actually said, "It was clear...." Still, he couldn't be talking about her, could he? She tried to focus as he continued to speak, his voice strong and confident. His entire body language showed that he knew what he was talking about.

"What would you say to such a woman, my friends? What would you share with her to let her know that she is focusing on the wrong things in life? I wish I could tell you that I was able to impart the word of the Lord into her spirit that same day, and that she realized the error of her ways and repented on the spot, but that is not what happened. Why? Frankly, brothers and sisters in Christ, I was not prepared then, but I am now. For her soul's sake, I had hoped she would have accepted my invitation to come to this Bible study tonight, but it appears that she—like so many women of my generation—would rather spend her time enhancing her outward appearance than seeking spiritual growth."

Claire felt her left eyebrow heading towards her hairline. As a "woman of his generation," she couldn't help but wonder if Robert Marsden had prepared this Bible study specifically for her and all her kind. She wasn't sure if she should be offended on behalf of all women around Robert's age, but she was convinced that if the 'wanna-be first lady' he'd mentioned had turned up tonight, she would definitely take offense. This was going to be interesting.

Robert opened his Bible just as the first scripture—First Peter 3:1-12—appeared on the projector screen.

"Now, to give you a bit of background, in the previous chapter, the author who identifies himself as Peter the Apostle, speaks about the importance of followers of Christ being submissive—citizens being submissive to governments and servants being submissive to masters. This third chapter begins with a discussion of ways in which wives should be submissive to their husbands.

"If you'll turn your attention to the first verse, you'll see where Peter advises wives to be submissive to their husbands so that if those husbands are not themselves believers, they will be won over to the Lord's side by the conduct of their wives. Even though he uses the word *fear* here, it is to be taken as reverential fear—a kind of awe akin to the fear we feel of God—rather than a fear of being abused or punished. Peter didn't want wives to be *afraid* of their husbands; he wanted them to be in *awe* of them. Then he goes on to speak about those wives being careful to ensure that their beauty radiates from the inside and is not merely a result of something that is applied to the skin and hair. The kind of beauty the wife should exhibit, therefore, is what he calls 'the unfading beauty of a gentle and quiet spirit.' He goes on to explain that the *holy women* of old invested in their inner beauty—their submission, their quiet calmness, their gentleness—and not in their looks."

Claire had started taking notes, but the more he spoke, the less she wrote. She sat there, her pen hovering over the page, waiting for something she figured she might actually want to remember. As Robert spoke about all the things contemporary women were doing to their bodies, she capped the pen and lay it on the book. *This guy is a real piece of work!* she mouthed silently.

He then referred to the scripture from the book of First Timothy, before saying, "We live in an age, Christian brothers and sisters, where so much attention is paid to our outward appearance that many of us—even Christians—fail to invest in what's on *the inside* of us. Christian wives need to be different. And if they are, Peter goes on to advise the husband how he should live with such a wife.

"Now, I want to make it clear that I am *not* in the market for a wife; I don't even want a girlfriend—as I mentioned before, I have too much going on to take on that kind of responsibility any time soon—but if I *were* looking for a life partner, I would seek to be the kind of husband Peter describes: understanding, honorable and strong. And I would want to be that husband for a woman whose beauty shines from the Holy Spirit residing inside her, and not beauty that's bought and sold in a store.

"Like Saint Paul, I want to make it clear that I desire 'that women clothe themselves in modest clothing, with decency and self-control, not with braided hair, gold, pearls, or expensive clothing, but with good works, which is proper for women professing godliness.' And let me tell you this, brothers and sisters, I wouldn't want a woman like the one I saw on Saturday—a woman so caught up in her appearance that she has to be perfectly made-up while taking her dog for a walk, but cannot make it to Bible study to hear the word of the Lord imparted to her! That kind of woman would be even *less* than my last resort; I'd rather remain single for the rest of my life than be with a woman who is so obsessed with outward appearance.

"I hope what I've shared will resonate in your spirit and have a positive impact on your life. Thank you."

℘

The blood rushing in Claire's brain was so loud that it drowned out the smattering of polite applause. She swallowed hard, trying and failing to overcome the unprecedented level of anger rising within her. She was so outraged that she jumped to her feet and rushed to gather her belongings. She could see Robert making the rounds between the rows, smiling and shaking the hands of those who had come to hear him speak. She needed to leave before he noticed her and the two elderly ladies sitting in the back of the room. She wasn't sure she could convince her tongue to stay saved in the presence of this man who had not only judged her so harshly but had actually made her the center of a Bible study! She made up an excuse about needing to get to bed early, and quickly ushered Aunt Ruby and Aunt Emmy through the door at the rear of the room and back to her car.

She gunned the engine so hard that her tires actually squealed as she made her way out of the parking lot.

Aunt Ruby, who was sitting beside her in the front, made a show of clicking her seatbelt into place with her left hand, while holding on to the dashboard with her right.

"In a big hurry, dear?" she asked without a hint of concern.

"A bit," Claire tried to smile, but she was glad the interior of the car was dark and Aunt Ruby couldn't see the unconcerned mask that was slipping out of place.

"That young man has a great future ahead of him, don't you think, Ruby? He's very confident," Aunt Emmy said from the back seat.

"He sure is, Emmy, but he also has a lot to learn."

Aunt Emmy responded, "Well, that's why he's in seminary, honey. At least the faculty who were in attendance will be able to show him where he went wrong in his presentation tonight so that he won't make the same mistakes going forward."

"Yes, that's true. With his charm and that voice, he's the kind of speaker that could read the dictionary to me and I'd sit and listen, but for those same reasons, he's got to be careful what he says. He could easily lead people astray by saying things without putting a lot of thought and prayer into his words. He is in the right place, though, for guidance and leadership. Let's keep praying for him."

"You all right, honey?" Aunt Emmy asked Claire as they made their way back to the other side of Jacksonville.

"Um-hmm," Claire began, but then remembered she was talking to someone old enough to be her mother. "Yes, ma'am... Aunt Emmy. I'm just not feeling very well at the moment. I'll be fine."

"Okay, sweetie. You make sure to make a nice cup of chamomile tea when you get home, ya hear?"

"Yes, Aunt Emmy. I will." She realized she was gripping the steering well so tightly she might develop calluses, so she relaxed a little.

Claire dropped Aunt Emmy off first. Afterward, she took Aunt Ruby to her house a couple of blocks from the bookstore. As Aunt Ruby gathered her purse, she thanked Claire for driving them.

"Of course, Aunt Ruby." Claire mustered up enough energy for a half-smile, but she knew it would probably be a while before she went back to the bookstore. If she ever did.

CHAPTER SEVEN

At home, Claire Foxwood did something she rarely ever did at nine o'clock on a Monday night. She drew herself a bath, to which she added a generous handful of lavender bath salts, hoping the scent would calm her aggravated nerves. As she sank into the warm water, she remembered Aunt Emmy's advice about the chamomile tea, but she wasn't much of a tea drinker and she only kept peppermint and ginger on hand in the event of a stomach ache.

As she let the water cover her body, she was surprised to find her cheeks wet with tears. She wasn't even sure why she was so upset. Was it because that... *that man* had judged her so harshly? Was it because he had the nerve to talk about her shortcomings in front of an audience? Was it because he had hinted—no, stated outright!—that she was attracted to him because she wanted to be first lady of his future church? How dare he? *How dare he?!*

The more she thought about it, the more upset she became. She could feel herself grinding her back teeth and had to force herself to relax her facial muscles. She'd end up with a migraine if she didn't relax. *The nerve of that man!*

She had his phone number. She had, of course, saved it when he'd sent her the address of the seminary by text message. She should call him and let him have it! She noticed her clenched fists and again forced herself to try and relax a little. She wouldn't call him. Not like this. If she unleashed her very justified fury on him, he'd no doubt classify her as another 'mad black woman' and find some way to dissect her behavior in a future sermon or Bible study. She *needed* to calm down. She *needed* to stop all this silly crying.

After half an hour, she got out of the bath and toweled herself dry. Sitting on the edge of her bed, she massaged lotion into her skin and tried to think of something... anything other than the whole situation.

Her phone pinged and she looked at the screen. It was a text message. From *that man*.

I didn't see you at Bible study tonight. Pity. Maybe you would have learned something.

She dropped the phone as without warning, the tears of anger and frustration that had finally morphed into tears of shame. The hands so recently clenched in anger were now hiding her contorted face. She wasn't the type of woman to cry often, but when she cried, she *cried*. And the more she cried, the more annoyed she became with herself for crying for reasons she didn't think she even understood.

Could it be that she was upset because *that man* was—on some level—*right*? Was it the conviction of the Holy Spirit that was making her react in such an emotional manner? Could there be even the smallest hint of truth in what he had said?

She'd been going to church her whole life, but she'd only gotten saved a little under a year ago, and she hadn't read all the way through her Bible yet. After going to the altar during an altar call, she'd been advised to read the book of John first, and then the other three gospels, and she'd done so. Since then, she read her devotional guide every morning before starting her day—except Sundays, when she'd be in church anyway—and it always focused on a particular scripture, so she'd probably read quite a bit of the Bible. But at no time in the last year had she come across the scriptures *that man* had preached about today. She wouldn't have forgotten them, not when she made her living as a makeup artist.

Knowing that trying to sleep would be futile, Claire headed into the living room to retrieve the Bible and notebook from the tote bag she had dropped on the dining table when she'd come home. She had only managed to write down the two scriptures and a couple of points, all intentions of note-taking suspended when she heard the diatribe *that man* had launched against the *wanna-be first lady* she later found out was none other than herself.

With her back against the headboard of her queen-sized bed, she skipped through the pages to First Peter, and was surprised to see that her hands were trembling. She was quite nervous about what she was going to read. Was she about to confirm that her work—what she had thought was her life's calling—was actually something that a Christian woman like herself was expected to condemn instead of condone?

There it was in plain English, "Do not let your adornment be merely outward—arranging the hair, wearing gold, or putting on fine apparel—rather let it be the hidden person of the heart, with the incorruptible beauty of a gentle and quiet spirit, which is very precious in the sight of God." She closed her eyes and leaned her head back against the headboard. What did this mean?

She looked at the notebook to remind herself of the second scripture and had to search the index to find the book of First Timothy. She could never remember which books of the Bible were from the Old Testament and which were from the New.

There it was again, the same message in different words, and apparently from a different writer. "I desire therefore that the men pray everywhere, lifting up holy hands, without wrath and doubting; in like manner also, that the women adorn themselves in modest apparel, with propriety and moderation, not with braided hair or gold or pearls or costly clothing, but, which is proper for women professing godliness, with good works."

What could she conclude based on these two verses? That a woman's attentions should be poured into professing godliness, with good works; that a woman shouldn't braid her hair or wear jewelry or expensive clothes; that she should be modest. What did all that mean, anyway?

Claire's conscience was racked with guilt. She *liked* dressing up. She *liked* the versatile styles into which she got her hair braided every now and then, and Lord knows, she loved not having to deal with it much for six weeks or so! Her mother had given her pearl earrings for her sixteenth birthday, a matching bracelet when she turned eighteen, and finally the full string pearl necklace at twenty-one. It was a complete set, and she liked wearing it. She enjoyed not only *wearing* makeup, but showing other women how to enhance their natural beauty with various products. In fact, she'd always considered it a real art.

"My God!" Claire found herself saying out loud as she thought about her clothes... her jewelry... her entire store. "Why didn't You tell me, Father? Why didn't You show me this before now? What am I supposed to do now? Am I supposed to close my business down? Burn my clothes and my jewelry? Stop getting my hair done? What now, Lord? *What now?*"

CHAPTER EIGHT

Claire sat in her car contemplating whether she should go into the bookstore or beat a hasty retreat. After all, one of the huge bookstores in the mall was likely to have the same devotional journal she'd seen in Notes in the Margin. They stocked just about everything in those bigger stores; it might take a longer time to find it, and it would probably be difficult getting an actual human being to help her, but surely it was there. Should she take her chances that *that man* was not in the store in front of her that day?

She scoped out the parking lot, looking for the car he'd been driving that day she had batted her eyelashes at him and somehow given off the vibe that she was interested in him only because he was a future pastor. She felt her jaw tighten up and knew that she wasn't fully over the whole situation. She sucked her teeth, and even though she was alone in the car, she could almost hear her mother scolding her for her poor manners. She really hoped she didn't see *that man* today. She wasn't big on confrontation, but when she got mad enough, she could hold her own in any quarrel.

A few deep breaths and a whispered prayer later, she stepped into the bookstore and took a quick look around. As was usually the case when she visited, Aunt Ruby was at the cash register at the front of the store reading a book. As the wind chimes over the door tinkled, the older woman looked over her glasses to see who had come in. Claire felt the warmth of Aunt Ruby's smile from all the way across the room. She might be all kinds of mad at *that man*, but she hoped she could maintain her relationship with Aunt Ruby and her sister. There was something about her that Claire was drawn to and admired immensely. She hadn't spent much time with them, but she could tell that Aunt Ruby and Aunt Emmy had been given the best names; they were both true gems.

"Claire, my dear! How are you?" came the greeting.

"I'm fine, thank you, Aunt Ruby. And you?" She walked over to the counter. She'd already taken a quick look and was convinced that *that man* wasn't around.

"I've been better, and I've been worse, sometimes in the same day." Aunt Ruby grinned cheekily.

"I hear you," Claire smiled, not sure how to respond.

"You look... different," Aunt Ruby observed. Claire had wondered if she was going to mention the change in her appearance. She was only wearing moisturizer and lip balm, as had become her habit since the day after the Bible study. She felt weird going to work in a store full of makeup when she wasn't wearing any herself. She hoped she looked fresh-faced and dewy, but inside she felt like she was living a lie. How could she, in good conscience, sell and 'upsell' products she no longer used herself? How could she convince women that makeup made them gorgeous when she now believed that it was something that made God frown? How could she profit off promoting sinful behavior in others? Still, she had to keep it real. She needed the money, and her store was her only source of income at the moment. She'd keep it open until she was clear what she needed to do.

"Yes, well..." Claire wasn't sure what to say, so she let the sentence hang in mid-air.

Aunt Ruby reached for a bookmark and slipped it between the pages of the book she'd been reading.

"Were you not at work today?" She looked pointedly at Claire's black polo shirt bearing the Outside-In logo.

"Yes, I was. I take the afternoon off every Wednesday."

"I... see...."

Claire could tell that Aunt Ruby didn't really "see," but she didn't want to prolong the discussion, so she figured a quick change of subject was in order.

"Last time I came in, I noticed a devotional journal. Do you know if you still have it?" It was no longer on the display table in the middle of the sitting area to the front of the store, and Claire wasn't sure if she should look for it in the Devotionals or Journals section of the store.

"A devotional journal, you say?"

"Yes. I don't remember the exact name, but it definitely said 'Devotional Journal' on the front. Last time I came in, it was right here." She pointed to the low coffee table that doubled as a display stand.

"Let me just have a look in this computer thing-y. Robert has been trying to teach me how to go through the inventory from the counter rather than going to the shelves. I guess now is as good a time as any to see if I've learned anything." Aunt Ruby looked over her glasses at Claire, which was no easy feat, considering how large the frames were. "I keep telling him you can't teach an old dog like me new tricks, but he's as stubborn as I am."

Claire didn't respond. She didn't want Aunt Ruby to lose her evidently high opinion of her, and there was something about *that man* that definitely rubbed her the wrong way these days. She didn't care too much that he was right about the scripture; what hurt was the way he'd made an example of her instead of raising his concerns with her directly. She tried hard to focus on Aunt Ruby instead of a man who wasn't even in the room.

"Ah, yes. Here we go. There's a couple of them in the Journals section. Maybe you'll see the one you're looking for." The older woman got down from her stool and made her way towards the bookshelves.

Claire followed her and watched as she withdrew four or five titles. "Here you go, darling. Was it one of these?"

Claire didn't think she saw the one she'd noticed earlier, but she took the stack of books from Aunt Ruby and moved towards the counter. "I'll just have a look." As she thumbed through each one, she noted the similarities and differences.

"I don't think it was any of these. The one I saw had an actual scripture for each entry. Each of these references one or two verses, but I want one that has the scripture copied right there, so I don't have to switch back and forth between my Bible and the devotional."

Aunt Ruby was on the same side of the counter as Claire, her hip leaning against it.

"May I ask you something, Claire?"

"Of course." Claire generally hated when people asked permission to ask a question, but this was Aunt Ruby. She could ask Claire anything she wanted to—even a redundant question!

"How often do you read your Bible?"

"My Bible? Well, like I said, I read a devotional every day. And it has a scripture right there."

Aunt Ruby smiled, "That's not what I asked, dear. I mean your actual Bible."

Claire thought for a moment. "I take my Bible to church on the weekend."

"Yes, of course; that almost goes without saying. So I take it you don't crack it open between Sundays, then?"

Ouch! That was harsh! Claire almost said the words out loud but she stopped just in time. She knew Aunt Ruby didn't mean to hurt her. Besides, she was right.

"Well...." She wasn't sure what to say.

"Don't feel bad, Claire; it's a pretty common situation. How's your prayer life?"

Whoa! Aunt Ruby isn't pulling any punches. "I... I pray in the mornings, after I read the devotional."

"I see."

"And I pray before I go to sleep at night, and I say—"

"Grace? Before you eat?" Aunt Ruby took the words out of Claire's mouth. How did she know?

"Yes."

"Hmm." Aunt Ruby was thoughtful. "Are you dating anyone, my dear?"

Claire thought the change of subject to be a bit abrupt, but she answered anyway. "Not right now, no."

"But you *have* dated."

"I have." She wondered where Aunt Ruby was going with the conversation.

"And when you date someone, you spend a lot of time with them, no?"

"Yeah... I mean, yes, of course. To get to know them." The woman she was talking to might be her friend, but she was still old enough that her very age demanded respect.

"Well, honey, how do you ever expect to get to know The Man Upstairs if you don't spend lots of time with Him?"

"What do you mean? I do my devotion every day except Sunday, when I'm going to—"

"Church." Again, Aunt Ruby preempted Claire by using the exact word she had been about to utter.

Claire smiled.

"And when you do your devotion, do you spend some quiet time afterward?"

"Well, no. I do it before I get ready in the morning, so I don't—"

"Have the time." Aunt Ruby smiled again, and Claire instinctively knew that this was the smile Aunt Ruby reserved for small children who didn't quite understand what was going on in the world.

"Claire, honey, I don't want to tell you how to live your life, but you don't get as old as I do—you don't serve God as long as I have—without picking up some important lessons along the way. Now I won't tell you what to do, but here's what *I* do: when I wake up in the morning, the first thing I do is tell God thanks for waking me up. I won't lie, some days, I ask Him *why* He woke me up! All these aches and pains... you know? Then I go to the bathroom before heading straight to the kitchen for my coffee—an extra dark roast with a few grains of salt to cut the bitterness—and I gather up my books right there on the kitchen table."

"Books?"

"Yes. I have a couple of devotionals I read, but I always keep my Bible and my journal close at hand. I use the journal to write down my thoughts about the scripture and the devotional entry. And I always spend some of that morning devotion time in prayer. And after I pour out my feelings, my concerns, my requests, my praise, my worship to the Lord, I wait."

"You wait?" Claire was curious.

"Yes. For an answer."

"To what?"

"To my prayers, dear."

"Do you mean to tell me that God actually answers your prayers? Every day?"

"Not at all, honey. But there are times when He speaks to me, and I've found that, in my experience, He speaks more when I am silent. God has good manners, you know! He won't talk while my mouth is flapping!" she chuckled.

Claire smiled, "I suppose. So do you hear, like, an audible voice?"

"No, although Emmy says she does. I get more of a *feeling*... an unction in my spirit."

"And what does He tell you?"

"It depends on what I need to hear, I suppose. Sometimes He gives me a direct answer to a yes-or-no question. Sometimes He gives me a scripture I need to meditate on. Sometimes He shows me someone in my mind's eye... someone I should minister to in some way or other. He does what needs to be done." Aunt Ruby looked over her glasses at Claire. "Now I'm not saying this is what you should do; this is a *description*, not a *prescription!*"

This time Claire joined in the chuckling. She had to admit that Aunt Ruby was a witty one.

"And sometimes He tells me something that's going to happen in the future... something I should look for... a sign that He's involved in something. I have visions I wrote down years ago that still haven't happened yet, but I look forward to them with joyful anticipation."

Claire was fascinated. She didn't realize God was still speaking to regular people. Since getting saved, she'd always thought He only spoke to ministers and deacons and other religious leaders, certainly not to the people who sat in the middle pews of the church.

"Another thing I do," Aunt Ruby began, and Claire knew she was still in teaching mode, "is to always read the verses in context. I don't just read the verse recommended for that day, but I read either the whole chapter or several chapters so I can understand the verse completely."

Claire didn't say anything, but she felt her brow wrinkle.

"It's very important to me to know what the writer had to say before and after any particular verse I'm studying. People often quote verses out of context, you know. For example, people always say Jesus said, 'An eye for an eye and a tooth for a tooth.' They use the verse to justify revenge. But they're only quoting the scripture in part. What He actually said was something like, 'You have heard it said, "an eye for an eye and a tooth for a tooth," but I tell you do not resist an evil person.' And that's when he says we should turn the other cheek. All of that is in the fifth chapter of Matthew. So if you only believed what people said, you'd think Jesus was advocating vengeance, when in reality, He was speaking against it."

"I see." It had never occurred to Claire that people might misquote the Bible. "But who would want to misquote the Bible?" Claire wondered out loud.

"In most cases, I don't think people really *intend* to mislead others; it's just what they're used to hearing. But the Bible encourages us to study to show ourselves approved. In my personal opinion, I've got to study the Word for myself. If I depend on the interpretation of others, I might be misled, and it would be no one's fault but my own. It's different, I suppose, in those parts of the world where the Bible isn't allowed, but here, we have access to the same information as our ministers do, and we just don't seem to use it."

"I see." Claire was beginning to feel like a broken record.

"Even when I go to church and Bible study, I make it a point to study the scriptures afterward and read everything —"

"In context," Claire chorused with her.

"Exactly! And I make sure to pray before and after that the Lord will reveal His meaning to me, that He'll help me to understand everything, and that He'll speak to me through His Word," Aunt Ruby smiled. "Anyway, dear, I do tend to go on and on. You take some time and look through those journals. Maybe you'll find one that speaks to you." She headed back to the other side of the counter and hopped onto the stool.

Claire leafed through the books again before selecting one that she felt would meet her needs. It didn't have the full scripture, but there were several recommended verses for every entry.

"Have you read the entire Bible, Aunt Ruby?"

"Several times, dear; several times. And it never ceases to amaze me that God will reveal a different part of Himself to me through verses I've already read over and over. He's an awesome, amazing God, you know. He delivers just what we need, exactly when we need it."

"Um-hmm," Claire replied absentmindedly, the wheels in her head turning. "Is there a particular Bible you recommend?"

"A Bible? Well, to be honest, I'm partial to the King James Version, myself, but I understand that the highfalutin' language—all those *thees* and *thous* and *thys*—might not appeal to you younger folk. I think you should choose a version that uses language you can understand easily. Whatever version you get, you might want to think about investing in a study Bible, one that has snippets of information that help the reader to understand the prevailing conditions at the time. Society back then was so different from society today, you know. It helps when the research has been compiled for you. A concordance is another good investment, and there are several Bibles that have both."

Claire winced when she learned the price of the study Bible with the concordance in the back of it, but judging by the weight of the book, it was probably worth every penny. She decided to keep using the Bible she already had and save so she could eventually buy the study Bible with the concordance.

As she thanked Aunt Ruby and headed toward the door, the other woman said, "Remember to pray, Claire. Develop a habit of talking to God. No matter what is going on in your life, make sure you make time to talk with Him, and then make sure you *listen*. And one last thing before you go, Claire—there's a saying that goes, 'The road to hell is paved with good intentions.'"

Claire stopped and pivoted on her heel. "I've always wondered what that proverb means, Aunt Ruby. I mean, if someone has good intentions, then shouldn't they be on their way to Heaven?"

Aunt Ruby smiled. "Heaven is not for those with good *intentions*, my dear. Heaven is for those who are saved by the blood of Jesus. But let's imagine that Heaven was for those who did good. If all we have is good *intentions*... if we never get around to actually following through on those intentions, then that's all they are—intentions."

Claire thought about it for a moment. "So are you saying that having a good motivation isn't enough?"

"What I'm saying is that sometimes our motivation is good and our heart is in the right place, but our actions might actually achieve the opposite effect. It happens to the best of us," she said enigmatically, "even pastors... and future pastors."

Claire's mouth fell open but at that moment, the wind chimes sounded as someone pushed the door. She whipped her head around, hoping it wasn't *that man*....

ଔ

"Hi, Aunt Ruby."

The middle-aged woman punctuated the greeting with a sigh, and Claire couldn't help but think that her voice sounded as if the very weight of the world was on her shoulders.

"Don't go yet, Claire," Aunt Ruby said before she smiled at the woman whom Claire didn't know. "Welcome, my dear Nalene. How are you doing?" Before she answered, Aunt Ruby waved her arm towards Claire and continued, "Do you know Claire Foxwood?"

The woman plastered a smile on her face as she looked at Claire, but it didn't quite reach her eyes. Again, Claire felt as if the woman was very burdened. It was as if Claire could almost sense a heaviness in her chest area. She wasn't familiar with the sensation, and she wondered what it was about this woman that was causing this reaction.

"No... at least, I don't think so." The stranger reached for Claire's hands and held them in a way Claire would have expected a much older woman to do. "I'm Nalene Betancourt."

"Claire Foxwood," was all Claire could say before Aunt Ruby chimed in.

"Nalene is the director over at the community center near to my church."

"Oh, is she?" Claire asked Aunt Ruby.

"Yes. Claire is a faithful customer, Nalene. She likes the same kinds of books as you—cozy mysteries and clean romance."

Nalene smiled again, but Claire could sense that she wasn't particularly interested in her reading habits.

"What's got you looking so down, Nalene? You usually come in with a pep in your step." Concern was printed on Aunt Ruby's face.

"Yes, well, one of our volunteers just told me she's leaving Jacksonville, and I just don't know what I'm going to do. No one wants to work with that group of girls."

"Which group?" Aunt Ruby asked.

"You know that on Saturdays we have volunteers from the community—teachers, business people, pastors and such—come in to work with different groups, right?"

"Yes, I remember you came to my church and made an appeal for volunteers." Aunt Ruby nodded as she spoke.

"Well, we have all sorts of groups coming in. From preschoolers to high school seniors. There's some older teen girls who come in, and I'm pretty sure their parents send them so they can be somebody else's problem for a while. They don't really want to be there, and I know for sure they don't want to actually learn anything. They were just warming up to Teriann. She's a fashion designer, so she was teaching them to do some of that stuff, but now she's leaving and I don't know what we're going to do." Nalene sighed so hard the book markers near the cash register shifted on their stand.

Suddenly, she turned to Claire, "You don't know anything about fashion design, do you?"

Claire shook her head. "Sorry, I don't."

Aunt Ruby pursed her lips. "Surely you can find something else than teenage girls are interested in."

"We probably could, but it'll be difficult. Teriann had started working on a fundraiser and everything. Now she's been offered a job in one of those major fashion houses in New York. It's just one more thing to worry about, you know."

"I remember you saying your funding had been cut."

"Yes, and we need a breakthrough soon, or we're going to have to start cutting programs. If it wasn't for businesses like this one, we'd probably have done that already."

"Speaking of which, I have your books right here. How's your back, Claire? Could you come pick up this box back here?"

"Okay." Claire put down her bag and joined Aunt Ruby behind the counter. The older woman pointed at a box on a shelf below the register, and Claire lifted it up with a grunt. It was heavier than she'd thought.

"I'm sure you've noticed that we have a read-and-return program, Claire. If you bring back your books after you're done, you get a credit worth thirty percent of what you paid for the book. Some of them we sell in the back of the store, and others we donate to the center."

"Would you mind just taking that to my car, Claire?" Nalene asked. "I can't take it... I have problems with my sciatica."

"No problem." Claire was glad to help.

Claire waited while Nalene turned back to Aunt Ruby. "Please give Robert my thanks, Aunt Ruby, and let him know the boys would love for him to come back again soon. I know he's busy, but whenever he has the time..."

"Of course, my dear. I'll call you in a couple of weeks when we have another box."

"Thank you. And if you can think of anyone who could help out with those girls at the center, please give them my card."

"Will do. God bless and keep you!"

"Nalene, could you just grab my bag? It was good talking with you, Aunt Ruby. I'm going to head home now. See you!"

Nalene retrieved Claire's bag of purchases and held the door open for her while she walked out. At Nalene's car, they bid each other goodbye and Nalene got in and drove away.

In the parking lot, Claire pondered what Aunt Ruby had meant by her last statement before Nalene had come in. What was it she had said? Something about *future pastors* having good intentions that sometimes led them to hell? Clearly, she'd been referring to *that man*, but what exactly had she been trying to tell Claire?

As a dark sedan pulled into the spot directly beside hers, Claire looked over and noticed *that man* sitting in the driver's seat. Without making eye contact, she quickly got into her car, fired up her engine and reversed out of the spot. She wasn't ready to talk to him again. There was something she needed to do first.

CS

"Was that Claire Foxwood I just glimpsed in the parking lot?" Robert asked Aunt Ruby as he stepped through the door.

"Why do you ask? Do you care?" Aunt Ruby was looking at him with a twinkle in her eye.

"Care? Of course not! I was just curious. She didn't take you and Aunt Emmy to Bible study like she said she would, and she didn't respond to my text message asking why."

"She was there. We all were." Aunt Ruby frowned.

Robert found that hard to believe. He'd been so busy the last week or so that he hadn't even thought to follow up with Aunt Ruby till now. "You were? But I didn't see you."

"We were sitting way in the back. Emmy was cold—like always—so we sat in the very last row, where it's usually warmer."

Robert's brow furrowed. "So why didn't she text to say she'd been there? I sent a message asking her about it later that night."

"You sent her a text message? And she didn't respond? Do you mind me asking what your text message actually said, honey?"

Robert wasn't sure why Aunt Ruby was so curious, but he shrugged, reached for his phone and scrolled through his sent messages. He didn't have many, as he wasn't a huge fan of texting. He preferred to save both his time and energy and make a phone call rather than send a text, but he didn't feel comfortable calling Claire. It wasn't like they were friends or anything, and he didn't want to send her the wrong message or encourage her. He could never imagine himself with her or anyone remotely like her. She was way too concerned about her looks. Claire Foxwood certainly had a lot of changing to do if she ever expected to catch the interest of a blood-washed man of God like he was.

"Ahem." Aunt Ruby caught his attention.

"Oh, yes. Here's the text right here. It says, 'I didn't see you at Bible study tonight. Pity. Maybe you would have learned something.'"

Aunt Ruby made a weird clucking sound in her throat while shaking her head and turning her attention back to her book.

"What's that for? Did I say something wrong?" Robert knew her disapproval when he heard it.

"Robert, may I ask you something personal?" She stuck a book marker between the pages.

"Sure. It's not like you haven't done that before!" he chuckled.

"True. That woman you mentioned at Bible study... was it Claire you were talking about?"

Robert didn't see any reason to hide the truth from Aunt Ruby. "As a matter of fact, it was."

She made the sound again, shaking her head all the while and looking at him with what seemed to be a mixture of pity and disgust.

"What?" He felt his defenses rising. What was Aunt Ruby not saying? "Out with it!"

"My dear, dear, boy. You have so much to learn."

She opened the book and started to read with her full attention, but Robert couldn't let a statement like that one go unexplained.

"What did I do?"

Aunt Ruby marked her page again and leaned forward on folded arms.

"Robert, please tell me you did not invite that young woman to come hear a Bible study that was all about her."

"I did not invite that young woman to come hear a Bible study that was all about her," Robert responded dutifully.

"Thank God. I didn't think you were that clueless."

Ignoring her statement, Robert continued, "I invited her to come hear a Bible study I hadn't written yet. It was *after* I invited her that I decided what I was going to talk about. And it just happened to be her. So I didn't invite her for that purpose; it just worked out that way in the end."

There it was again—the head-shaking and throat-clucking.

"What?" He hunched his shoulders and raised his hands in a questioning manner.

"Robert, I don't want you to take this the wrong way, but sometimes you men can be so *dumb!*"

Huh? How could he not take that the wrong way? She had just insulted his intelligence. He swallowed what he'd like to say and looked into her eyes. "I'm *sure* I don't know what you're talking about, Aunt Ruby."

"Now, don't go getting all defensive on me. I'm getting old, and I don't care as much as I used to about preserving someone else's feelings. Let me give it to you straight: I don't think there's anything wrong with planning a study about something someone said or did, but to go on stage and talk about someone you expect to be sitting in the audience... well, what exactly did you expect to accomplish?"

"I *expected* her to do some introspection, see where she's going wrong and change her ways. And I'm almost sure something has changed... she didn't have that layer of war paint on just now. Clearly, something I said struck a nerve with her! And I wasn't wrong, Aunt Ruby, the scripture clearly says..."

"You know, honey," Aunt Ruby cut in, "my concern at this point in time is not about how right or wrong your interpretation of the scripture was—"

My interpretation? Robert almost voiced the thought out loud, but he realized she was still speaking.

"—that's between you, God and your professors. I just don't like how you went about the whole thing."

Strange. His supervisor at the seminary had just mentioned something along the same lines an hour or two earlier, but their meeting had been cut short by a fire drill at the seminary. By the time they could go back into the building, Dr. Crouch had a class and they had agreed to meet in another few weeks.

"What do you mean?" He may as well ask Aunt Ruby. She may not be a college professor, but she'd lived long enough to have an opinion on just about everything, and it would be nice to have a response planned for Dr. Crouch in the event that he and Aunt Ruby were on the same track.

"There's a scripture that encourages God's servants to be gentle and to display humility when correcting people with opposing views to theirs. It's from Second Timothy."

"And you're saying that to say...?" Robert prompted her.

"The words speak about *humility* and not *humiliation*. It's a good trait in a pastor, my dear. What I'm saying is that there are things that should be done in private, and one of them is correction. In the future when you become a minister, I wouldn't recommend you get behind a pulpit and humiliate members of the congregation. You'd soon find yourself alone in that church."

Robert wasn't sure how to respond. "I wasn't trying to humiliate her, Aunt Ruby. I was merely trying to show her the error of her ways."

"According to whom?"

"According to God!" Robert's answer came out more harshly than he'd intended, and he noticed Aunt Ruby's eyebrows dart upwards.

"You mean according to *you*. You practically called the woman a harlot! You decided she was unworthy of your attention and that you would punish her for the audacity of being attracted to such a holy man as yourself when she clearly didn't meet your standards. So instead of rejecting her privately, in the very moment you became aware of the attraction you apparently don't share, you decided to use her."

"I most certainly did not!"

"Well, what do you call it, honey? You yourself said you didn't know what to focus on until she gave you the idea."

"The Bible is supposed to be a mirror, Aunt Ruby, to show us where we fall short. If she was convicted about her actions, then that is between her and God."

"Yes, my dear. You're absolutely correct. *The Bible* is a mirror; *you* are not. And you made it so that it was between her and God *and* you *and* the entire audience."

Robert felt his temperature rising. He did not want to lose his temper with a woman for whom he had boundless respect, so he took a deep breath before responding in what he hoped was an appropriate tone. "So, what do you think I could have done differently?" She was wrong, of course, but he didn't want to prolong the argument. Besides, he wanted to prepare himself in case Dr. Crouch was on the same erroneous path as Aunt Ruby.

"There are several things I might have done in your shoes. Chief among them—I would have talked to her in private. If it was something I thought could benefit the group, then I'd concentrate on the scripture and not the person. I'd think about how I'd feel in her shoes, and I would *not* have gone on stage and berated her."

Robert decided against defending himself. His experiences arguing with Aunt Ruby—and there had been quite a few arguments—told him he wasn't likely to win. "Okay, Aunt Ruby. I hear you."

"Promise me you'll think about what I've said. And that you'll meditate on Second Timothy... especially the last few verses of the second chapter. I think you'll find it most enlightening. And while you're at it, you might want to read

Romans two, especially the first three verses. Here, I'll write them down for you." She reached for a sticky notepad, made a few jottings and handed the square of paper to him.

"All right, Aunt Ruby. I will. My last class today was canceled, so I figured I'd come by. You can have the afternoon off if you'd like."

"Hmm. I think I'll just stay and finish reading this book." Aunt Ruby came around the counter and placed her hand on Robert's.

"Son, I love you, and I want you to be the best you can possibly be. You know that, don't you?"

Robert smiled and nodded. "Without a doubt."

She reached up to kiss his cheek and then headed toward the sitting area with her novel.

CHAPTER NINE

For the next few weeks, Claire Foxwood immersed herself in the Bible. At first, it was difficult to maintain her focus, and a couple of times she found herself waking up when she didn't know she'd been sleeping. Eventually, she began to look forward to reading it. The Word really was becoming like her daily bread. All her life, she had been hearing the popular stories of the Bible—about Adam and Eve in the Garden of Eden, about Jesus feeding the multitude, about His birth and His death on the cross—but now she was learning about people she'd never heard of before and people she'd never paid attention to. She was ashamed to discover that among the Psalms and Proverbs, among the letters Saint Paul had written, there were several books she'd never heard mention of before... books like Habakkuk, Micah and Zephaniah.

Before she even got to the end of Genesis, she was completely intrigued. She was convinced that the writers of long-standing soap operas could learn a thing or two about drama if they only read the story of Jacob and how Laban had tricked him into marrying Leah instead of Rachel. He had ended up maintaining two households, with two wives who were actually sisters, and he was encouraged by those wives to impregnate their respective maids. She'd never expected that kind of drama in *the Bible,* of all books!

As she read more and more about the people who lived during biblical times, she knew she was learning more and more about God and how He operated. Although contemporary society was markedly different, countless lessons remained the same. She found herself filling her journal quickly. She would write her thoughts about the situations she was reading about and what she was learning about herself in the process. She also enjoyed writing down her prayers. It would probably take her at least a year to read the entire Bible, and she was sure by then she would have finished several journals. Maybe she should sign up for some kind of subscription service to ensure that she always had one at hand.

Even though she was devouring the Bible, she had added the new activity to her schedule rather than replacing her daily devotions with Bible study. She was also following Aunt Ruby's own routine regarding how she went about starting her mornings with God. She'd started waking up half an hour earlier than she used to—which meant going to bed early, too— so that she could spend some time in God's presence before she started her day.

Within a couple of weeks, she could definitively say that the time she spent in devotion early in the morning was making a positive difference in her life. There were the mornings she overslept—usually because the night before she'd been caught up in a mystery novel she couldn't put down. Those were the days she rushed through her devotion, and those were the days she tended to get angrier in traffic, to snap at the slow cashier in the supermarket or to talk down to Mitzie in the store. When she had that 'God and me time,' she was generally an easier person to get along with.

Both the Bible reading and the time spent in devotion were eye-openers for Claire, but one scripture in particular had a resounding impact on her life and her lifestyle.

One Saturday morning, she was sitting in her recliner, her Bible and journal in her lap, a spill-proof mug of coffee in one hand and her devotional in the other, when she came across a scripture that without warning sent her mind straight back to her twelfth summer. At the time, she stood on the precipice of puberty and had been sent to spend the summer vacation with her grandmother.

Claire put down the Nancy Drew mystery she'd been reading and drained the glass of lemonade. She absentmindedly noticed the ring the glass had left on Grandma's end table. She never could remember to use a coaster.

Anticipating harsh words from her grandfather, she slid the homemade doily so that it was slightly off-center. Good. It covered the translucent ring that marred the finish and she hoped it would go away sooner rather than later.

After rinsing her glass at the kitchen sink, Claire stood there staring out the window, her left foot resting on top of her right. It was kind of strange to be looking at the small rectangular yard her grandfather did a great job of maintaining. She wasn't sure what kind of tree was out there, but it had low branches that were perfect for sitting in while she lost herself in yet another library book.

The view out the window was so different from her parents' apartment back in Chicago. They lived in a two-bedroom apartment, with all the windows facing a brick wall behind their building. There was no view unless she walked to the park a couple of blocks away. She loved being here in South Bend, Indiana, where her grandparents' bungalow was small enough to be cozy but big enough that they weren't falling over each other all the time.

And the best thing of all? When she spent summers with Grandy and Grandpa, she had a bathroom all to herself. No waiting till Daddy or Mommy got out so she could take a shower.

She moved out of the kitchen and down the hallway to the bedrooms. After knocking at her grandparents' bedroom door, she waited dutifully for a response. She'd only been there a couple of days but she had already been reminded of Grandpa's house rules. "Children should be seen and not heard. Speak when you're spoken to. Answer when you're called. Knock on a closed door and wait for a response. If you don't get a response, don't open the door unless it's a bathroom door, and only if you're about to make a puddle on the floor."

Claire was pretty sure Grandpa was on the porch, and she knew Grandy wasn't as much of a stickler for rules as her husband of some fifty-odd years, but Claire preferred to err on the side of caution. Grandpa's temper was legendary.

"Come in, Claire-my-dear." Her grandmother was getting old and rickety, as she liked to say, but she had a musical voice that tinkled in Claire's ear.

It was the first time Claire had gone into Grandy and Grandpa's bedroom, and she was greeted by a scent she later learned was the gardenia perfume Grandy would spray on the linens. Grandy was seated in a white ladder-back chair facing the vanity mirror with a few small brushes and open jars on a black velvet tray in front of her. When she turned towards her grandchild, Claire was amazed at how different she looked. It was as if she had dropped two decades of her seventy-plus years since she'd seen her only half an hour earlier.

"Grandy, you look so different!"

"Why, yes, my dear. I bet I sound different, too."

It was nothing short of remarkable. It was as if someone had waved a magic wand over her grandmother. Just before coming into the bedroom, she had said to Claire, "You're coming with me to the shupermarket, ishn't that right, Claire-my-dear? I'm going to get ready. Shee you in thirty minutesh or so." Yet here she was, her speech impediment miraculously gone.

"Well, yes, you do."

"I put my dentures in, honey." She flashed Claire a toothy grin and the child could see that she was, indeed, wearing a smile she hadn't had earlier. In the two days since her parents had dropped her off, Claire hadn't seen her Grandy with her false teeth in place. What a difference they made! It was as if they had lifted the elderly woman's whole face.

Claire watched, mesmerized, as Grandy applied something to her cheeks.

"What's that, Grandy?"

"It's blush, my dear. Makes the old girl look 'together,' doesn't it? Especially when I get my eye shadow and lipstick on."

"You wear makeup, Grandy?"

"I do. Doesn't your momma wear makeup?"

"Not really. She says she doesn't have anything against it, but she doesn't have time to get all dolled up when she has a child and husband to take care of."

"Well, I always say, 'To each his own,' but I am definitely the type to get all dolled up. I don't go out the door without my eye shadow and blush, honey! Maybe that's why I ended up with six children and your momma only has one—but don't tell her I said so." She winked, and Claire suspected Grandy had said something she shouldn't have.

"But why do you wear makeup, Grandy? You're already beautiful enough, especially with your teeth in." It was the truth. Now that Grandy had popped her dentures in, she could probably pass for sixty-five.

"It does Grandy's heart good to hear you say that, but I don't wear makeup to look beautiful."

"Why do you wear it then?" Claire genuinely wanted to know.

"Well, Claire-my-dear," Grandy lay her lipstick aside and turned to look at her granddaughter. "I wear makeup because it shows that I put a little thought into my appearance. I was born beautiful, but knowing that I look as good on the outside as I feel on the inside gives me a little extra pep in my step and lifts my spirits when they need lifting."

"Do they need lifting today, Grandy?"

"Not really, honey. My grandbaby is here, and you're all the spirit-lifting I need for the rest of the summer. Today, I just want to make your old granddaddy look twice. Gotta keep him interested, you know. Make him sit up and pay attention sometimes! Watch and see if

he doesn't end up driving us to the store." She launched into a fit of giggling that had Claire raising her eyebrows. Grown-ups! She'd never understand them!

"I'm glad I'm lifting your spirits, Grandy. I didn't know I could do that."

"Of course you can, honey! You know, the Bible talks about people having different gifts. Some people have the gift of teaching, some have the gift of preaching... there's all sorts of gifts. Your gift, my sweet grandbaby, is to lift people's spirits. I can't tell you exactly how I know that; it's just an unction I have deep down inside me. I don't know how you're going to do it, but you're going to reach people's hearts in a way that just makes them feel better about who they are. You, my sweetheart, make me feel good from the inside out, and you mark my words, honey, that gift is going to make room for you. It's going to open doors for you that no man can shut."

Claire looked down at the page and found the scripture again. It was from Proverbs 18. "A man's gift makes room for him, and brings him before great men." Is that what Grandy had been talking about all those years ago? Claire knew Grandy went to church, but she wasn't the type of woman who spouted a lot of scripture all the time. Not for the first time, she wished her grandmother was still around to explain some of the enigmatic things she had told Claire as a child.

Claire put the Bible and mug down and opened her journal.

Lord, years ago my Grandy told me that my gift would make room for me, and that my gift was making people feel good from the inside out. You know that I've heard that same phrase so many times since then. I heard it so much when I was at the insurance company, even when they were telling me why they didn't want to promote me. I heard it so often that I went and did that makeup artistry course, not so much because I wanted to help people to look good, but because I wanted to help them boost their self-confidence. Lord, I always figured that for some of us, we feel better when we think we look better. That's why I started Outside-In. I didn't even remember that Grandy told me my gift was making people feel good from the inside out. So what now, Lord?

Now I'm not sure where to go. What do I do when I own a makeup store and I go to Bible study and learn that it's wrong to promote wearing makeup? I'm trying to be a good Christian, Lord. The last thing I want to do is go to hell or—even worse—help other people get there! I would appreciate hearing a word from You, Lord, because I don't know what to do.

And while I wait to hear from You about that, Lord, I'd appreciate if You'd show me what my gift really is. I don't need to be before great people, Lord, but I do want to glorify You in any way I can.

She closed the book and her eyes and waited to see if the Lord would speak to her, but it seemed He was being particularly silent. All that kept resonating in her spirit was the scripture she'd read, "A man's gift makes room for him, and brings him before great men."

αβ

Claire stood in the doorway of Outside-In and smiled invitingly at the women who walked past. It had been an exceptionally slow day in the store, and she was losing hope that she would make any sales at all. She hadn't decided whether she was going to keep the store open just yet—she was still waiting for instructions from God—but while it was open, she had to pay both the rent and her assistant. She also needed to eat. And read.

She noticed a tall, middle-aged woman walking past and racked her brain trying to remember the woman's name. "Miss Nalene?" she tried. The woman looked up and smiled.

"I know you," she turned towards Claire, "you were in the bookstore with Aunt Ruby last week."

"Yes, I'm Claire."

"Right! Claire, I remember. Call me Nalene. What with all the kids at the center, I hear enough 'Miss Nalene' to drive me crazy," she smiled. "A friend of Aunt Ruby and Robert is a friend of mine. Do you work here?" She looked up at the sign over the door.

"Yes. This is my store, actually. Come on in! I'll treat you to a free mini-facial; my treat." Claire stepped aside and waved Nalene into the store.

"Really?"

"Of course. No offense, but you look like your spirit could use a little lifting." Claire wasn't sure what it was about this woman, but for the second time, being in her presence was causing Claire to feel heavily burdened. She wished there was some way she could lighten the load Nalene was so obviously carrying. If a facial mask and a neck and shoulder massage could do that, then she would be glad to offer the complimentary service.

She waved Mitzie away and took Nalene to the private consultation area of the store to do the service. During that time, she asked about Nalene's work at the community center and her earlier life in corporate America. Forty minutes later, Nalene looked refreshed and renewed.

As they stepped from behind the screen, a young woman who Claire recognized as a regular customer came through the door. She told them she had a special dinner date and that she was confident her boyfriend was going to propose.

"I wanted to look special… for the pictures, in case he really does pop the question tonight!"

"No problem," Mitzie smiled.

Nalene appeared intrigued. "Do you mind if I watch? I don't wear a lot of makeup, but I'm curious about how some of those looks are achieved."

The young woman smiled readily, her excitement contagious.

Nalene asked Claire a ton of questions as Mitzie applied primer, foundation, and a range of shadows and creams.

Claire chuckled. "You sound like you're studying for a test!"

"All this is fascinating." Nalene turned to Mitzie. "Where did you learn to do this?"

"I did a makeup artistry course, but even before that, I learned almost everything I know from Claire. She's a great teacher! She's gifted. When I came in here, I didn't know anything about makeup. All I knew was black eyeliner… I even used it on my lips!" She smiled ruefully, shaking her head. "I don't know what I'd be doing if it wasn't for her. She took a chance and hired me straight out of high school when nobody else wanted to."

"And I made the right choice, didn't I, Mitz? You've blossomed into a lovely young lady. I'm so proud of you."

Mitzie blushed and turned back to her client, who was waiting patiently.

Nalene turned to Claire, who could almost see the wheels turning in her new friend's head. "What?"

"You know, Claire, we didn't find anyone to replace Teriann at the community center. We offered fashion design because we thought it was something teenage girls might be interested in, but I think they'd be just as interested in learning about makeup. And if you could teach them a skill they could use to earn a little money, that would be icing on the cake!"

Claire wanted to decline immediately, but the hope coming alive in Nalene's eyes made her reconsider. "But I couldn't offer them certification or anything. I'm not a trained instructor."

"No worries. Right now, our focus is on teaching them practical skills that will enhance their lives. Certification can come later for those who want to pursue it."

"What kind of hours are we talking about, Nalene?"

"We could make some changes to accommodate your schedule, though it might take some rearranging. The girls come in every Saturday, but your session would be every other week. They're also doing a computer course in the same time slot."

"Perfect!" Mitzie chimed in. "You already take every other Saturday afternoon off."

Claire could have strangled her assistant, but there was the hope in Nalene's expression again. The woman looked transformed. "Promise me you'll think about it, Claire," Nalene pleaded.

"I'll think about it, but what about those times when we have an event or something?"

"We'll cross that bridge when we get to it, my dear Claire."

Claire nodded her head, then blinked her eyes rapidly when it almost seemed as if Nalene's face was morphing into her beloved Grandy's and her grandmother's voice rang in her ears.

"... *you mark my words, Claire-my-dear, that gift is going to make room for you.*" Now what could that possibly have to do with teaching girls about makeup application?

CHAPTER TEN

What felt like years after presenting his Bible study, Robert finally had the chance to sit down and meet with his adviser, Dr. Crouch, to discuss his presentation. He left the meeting less confident than he had been when he'd knocked on the door forty-five minutes earlier. He'd tried not to argue with the man whom he knew basically held his degree in his hand, but it had taken quite a bit of biting his tongue and counting to ten and back in several languages. He couldn't believe Dr. Crouch had almost given him a failing grade! The whole idea was preposterous!

Robert struggled to drag his attention back to his driving and noticed a few nanoseconds too late that there was a police cruiser behind him. In his rear-view mirror, he could see the lights flashing at the same time the wail of the siren just about pierced his eardrum. He turned his indicator on and pulled over to the side of the road. "Perfect! What next, Lord?" He heard himself say as he switched off his engine. He sat motionless as he waited for the officer to approach him. He smiled when the person he could see in his side mirror turned out to be a woman. Maybe if he was nice, she'd let him off with a warning.

"Good afternoon, Officer." He offered the greeting and what he hoped was a warm smile as soon as she stopped at his mirror.

There was no preamble. "License and registration, please."

"Yes, ma'am. Right away, ma'am." He retrieved the paperwork from his glove compartment and reached into his pocket for his wallet.

She took what he offered but did not return his smile. The wind was blowing her blond hair into her face, and Robert couldn't decide whether she was closer to twenty or thirty-five.

"Lovely weather we're having, Officer..." he glanced at the name tag on her chest, "... Officer Love."

"Mr. Marsden, do you know how fast you were going?"

"Well, Officer Love—is that your real name?"

"Mr. Marsden, let's be clear here: I'm not interested in you. I am not interested in the weather. What I *am* interested in is whether or not you know how fast you were going."

"Well, to be honest, I—"

She cut him off. "You were going seventeen miles per hour above the posted speed limit, Mr. Marsden. In a school zone."

"But school is—"

"Don't argue with me, Mr. Marsden. I don't take kindly to wrongdoers like yourself trying to argue your way out of consequences. And I especially don't appreciate your trying to flirt with me."

Robert opened his mouth to say, "I was only trying to be nice," but decided against defending himself. She clearly had the upper hand, and it was in his best interest to remember that. She had assumed he was flirting with her when all he'd been doing was trying to talk his way out of a ticket. It was ridiculous how quickly she had jumped to conclusions about him.

Five minutes later, he stuffed the car's documents and speeding ticket into his glove compartment and drove away slowly. Not only had she ticketed him, but she'd also made him wait while she ran his license plate, *and* she'd given him a lecture about assuming every woman who crossed his path was interested in him. *What a pill!* He thought. All her assumptions about him had been wrong, and she hadn't even given him a chance to defend himself.

The whole situation reminded him about the discussion he'd had with Dr. Crouch. He frowned so hard he could feel a headache coming on. He didn't even want to think about the meeting. Not yet, at least. Not till after he made it to the bookstore without another traffic ticket. He was supposed to relieve Aunt Ruby early so she could go to a meeting. He needed to relax before he saw her; as perceptive as she was, she would probably find out about the fine. And that would only lead to his third lecture for the day. He really wasn't up to another one.

∞

Robert felt only a little bit better by the time he got to the store, but he smiled at Aunt Ruby as he stepped through the door.

"Robert," she grinned as she gathered up her things, "you're right on time. Thanks for agreeing to the switch."

"Aunt Ruby, you're working here without taking a full pay check, just so I can get to school. Making these kinds of adjustments… well, that's the very least I could do."

"Which reminds me, honey, that next check that you're going to write for me… can you make it out to the community center instead of the food bank? I want to make my donation to the fundraiser early. There's still so much stuff that needs to be bought."

"No problem, Aunt Ruby. I don't know why you think you can afford to donate all your earnings. It can't be easy living on a fixed income."

"Don't worry about me and my income, son. I'm not as dumb as I look," she winked at him. "I've made some shrewd investments in my time. And my sweetheart took care of me when he passed away, so I'm doing okay. Unless I live to be older than a hundred and five. Then I might ask you to make the check out to me instead!" She laughed, as she always did when she made a joke, and stepped from behind the counter.

"So, where are you off to this afternoon?" Robert sifted through a stack of bills that had come in.

"The center, honey. I volunteered to help with the decorating. Today we're going to be sewing the curtains for the back of the stage. The fundraiser is this weekend, remember? You're planning to be there, aren't you? And remember you promised you would wear something other than jeans. Just for me." She batted her eyelashes and he couldn't help but chuckle. Aunt Ruby was something else!

"Yes, Aunt Ruby, of course." Robert hadn't remembered a thing about the event until she'd brought it up earlier, but he had promised to stop by after closing up the shop that coming Saturday.

"It's just wonderful how Claire stepped in and saved the day over at the center," Aunt Ruby said.

Robert could tell she was just pretending to look for something in that huge pocketbook she always carried. She was baiting him. He took a breath. She could bait all she wanted, but he was *not* going to bite the hook this afternoon; his day was already going pretty badly, and he didn't want her to get on his case about Claire and the Bible study.

He smiled and reached for a box of used books that needed shelving.

"Yes, sir," she continued, "she has been making *such* a huge difference in just a few weeks."

He dug deeper into the box, hoping she would take the hint and go away.

She didn't. "You know, they had a volunteer who was teaching the girls all about fashion design, and she had to leave. And Claire happened to be in here one day when Nalene came for her books, and the rest, as they say, is history. Claire is teaching a course a couple afternoons a month."

"Oh, really? Didn't know she was a teacher. What does she teach?" He was genuinely interested. What could a woman like Claire possibly share with a group of teen girls?

"Makeup application."

He huffed. "Makeup application? She really didn't learn a thing from the Bible study, huh?"

"I'm not sure she was the one who had something to learn from that Bible study."

Robert could feel yet another lecture coming on, so he was relieved when all she said was, "Are you familiar with the saying, 'Physician, heal thyself,' my dear?"

"Yes, Aunt Ruby."

"Let me leave you with something of a variation on that— Professor, teach thyself. See you tomorrow, dear."

And with that, she was gone, the wind chimes over the door signaling her exit.

Robert shook his head. What was it with her and Dr. Crouch? Was he too dense to figure out what they were saying to him? He still wasn't clear about where he had gone wrong with his Bible study. And he had definitely gone wrong *somewhere*—the grade he'd gotten was sure proof of that.

CHAPTER ELEVEN

Claire had been working on the fundraiser for weeks. She'd been spending almost every spare moment on it... so much so, that her reading was suffering. She hadn't picked up a book in the last two weeks, and she was only doing a chapter a day of her Bible. She was at the community center almost every evening after work, and all afternoon on Saturdays if the store wasn't too busy. Thank goodness the center was closed on Sundays, or she was sure she'd be there after church, too. She would be glad when this whole event was over.

She had been working with the group of fifteen- to seventeen-year-old girls for almost two months now. They had come in either overconfident for the wrong reasons or lacking in confidence. Many were rough around the edges, but she had worked patiently with them, and she was so proud of how far they'd come. She really hoped their friends and family members would be able to come to the fundraiser and see how they'd been spending their time lately. Maybe it would inspire some of them, too.

It was, in fact, an inspiration for her, as well. The more time she spent with the girls, the more evident it was that her makeup artistry was a gift the Lord had given her so that He could use her to reach others *for Him*. She had meditated on the chapters Robert had shared, and she had arrived at the conclusion that there was nothing wrong with wearing makeup, fancy hairstyles, or attractive clothes. The problem, she believed, was when these things became more important than developing a spirit that was pleasing to God. She had been praying and studying the Word, and she knew that she was a changed person. She liked makeup, enjoyed wearing it and showing others what it could do; but she didn't depend on it to make her feel better. She depended on the Lord who had created her. She placed her faith in Him every day and asked Him to help her to become more confident within herself, regardless of what was happening on the outside. She had also started wearing makeup again and was once again focusing on making her store a phenomenal success.

Over the past month or two, she could see where her changing attitude had begun to impact her interaction with the world around her. She was slowly making more and more changes, even at the store, and here at the center, her approach was to help the girls find their own inner beauty.

It was the evening of the fundraiser, and she and the others were as busy as proverbial bees backstage. The show would be starting soon. That week, Aunt Ruby, Claire and the other volunteers, as well as the young participants in the various programs, had transformed the auditorium, and she was very pleased with how well their vision had turned out.

She and the young ladies had had a dress rehearsal the night before, and everything had gone very well. They'd sought sponsorship from the local business community, and many had been glad to help, providing them with the material they needed to create the magic Claire had been teaching them. Outside-In was one of the sponsors, and Claire had even gone deep into her own pockets in her attempt to make everything as close to perfect as possible. Now, as she and Mitzie worked on one young lady after another, she prayed fervently that everything would go well that night. She would hate for the kids to be disappointed with any aspect of their performance.

She took a moment to peer through the curtains at the crowd that was assembling. They had gotten a lot of support, and she could recognize a few of the people in attendance. She had seen Aunt Ruby when she had arrived earlier, and several members of her church and some of her clients from the store had turned up, as well. There were dozens of other people out there. Great. The more people who came and saw what the youth programs at the center were helping people to do, the more volunteers they would have and the more young people they could reach. Maybe they could even drum up some more financial support from the business owners.

She let the curtain fall into place and went back to the chaos that was the dressing room. They had less than an hour before the curtain went up.

ଔ

Robert got to the community center a few minutes after seven o'clock. He had closed the store at six and followed Aunt Ruby's instructions to go home and change. He was surprised by the number of people he saw milling around in the parking lot, not to mention the crowd inside. Aunt Ruby hadn't told him exactly what was happening tonight, but he was more than willing to support community initiatives. He'd been donating used books to the center, but he didn't have enough time to come down as often as he'd like. He wasn't sure if this would be the neighborhood he would be preaching in, but he figured the more people he met in the community, the better it would be.

He stopped at the noticeboard close to the front door long enough to look at the event poster that had been put up. He felt a frown coming on. Among the expected song, dance and dramatic pieces, he saw that there was also going to be a teen fashion show. A furrow developed in his forehead. When would the adults who had an influence over young ladies and gentlemen stop leading them astray? When would they understand that the focus needed to be on developing what was inside of the body, rather than showcasing what was on the outside? He sighed. To satisfy Aunt Ruby, he'd stick around for a while, but he didn't plan on watching a fashion show. There were few things he detested more than bodies on display seeking earthly approval.

He paid for his ticket and stepped through the doors. Looking around, he thought he saw Aunt Ruby heading out of a side door. Remembering that she had promised to save him a seat, he moved in the same direction, hoping she hadn't just gone to the bathroom. *How awkward would that be?* he chuckled to himself.

He ducked through the doorway and found himself in a hallway that led to a single door at either the end of it. One was an emergency exit. The other door didn't have any restroom signs, so he walked briskly towards the door, knocked tentatively, and when there was no response, he pushed it open.

He hadn't expected to be greeted with sheer chaos.

It seemed he'd found himself backstage. There were dozens of people—most of them teenagers—engaged in various activities. In one corner, he identified a trio of girls practicing their harmonies. Not far from them, a boy who looked to be about fifteen or sixteen was playing a flute from sheet music. A couple of girls wearing long white leotards with long white skirts over them were going through some kind of warm-up exercises, their long limbs extending beyond the limits of normal human bodies. On the far side of the room, he observed Aunt Ruby, who was watching intently as a woman applied makeup to the face of a young lady of seventeen or eighteen. When the woman turned, he shook his head in disgust. It was none other than Claire Foxwood. He shouldn't have been surprised. The woman was clearly obsessed with her looks, and now she was passing that unhealthy, ungodly obsession on to the next generation. It was clear that she had learned nothing from attending his Bible study!

Aunt Ruby laughed at something Claire had said then turned towards him. Not wanting to be caught watching them, Robert ducked out the door and almost sprinted towards the auditorium.

He felt like leaving, but why? As he made his way to the back of the room, he took the time to analyze why Claire's involvement in a fashion show bothered him so much. He was more disappointed than he'd have liked to admit. The truth was, despite her flaws, he found her quite interesting.

With her warm eyes, high cheekbones and full lips, she was the kind of woman who was born beautiful. If only she could understand that her true beauty should shine from within. If only she were interested in studying her Bible and finding God's purpose for her life, the way he was doing. No wonder she hadn't responded to his text message that night; she hadn't benefited from being there *at all*.

He was still deciding whether or not to stay when he heard his name. He turned to see Aunt Ruby calling him over. He reluctantly turned and moved to join her as she stood close to the wall, but before he could open his mouth, the lights dimmed and the stage lights came on. She moved into a row of seats close to the front, and he saw that there was a seat available beside her. He didn't see Aunt Emmy, so he sat and returned the older woman's smile.

The first performance was a scene from a play about a teenage girl who was so desperate to be accepted by the popular kids at school that she was willing to do whatever it took for them to notice her. The storyline was not unfamiliar to Robert, but the playwright had made it more interesting by adding songs and incorporating off-stage voices that represented the battle between good and evil as it took place in the main character's mind. Robert was intrigued, and the scene ended so dramatically that he found himself wishing he could see the rest of it right away.

It was only then that the MC appeared close to the extreme right of the stage and announced that the complete play would be separated into three scenes, with the interlude between scenes being filled with other performances. Robert was so intrigued that he forgot about his desire to leave early.

During the first interlude, the audience was treated to performances of song and dance, as well as a brief set by the flautist Robert had noticed earlier. The kids were fantastic, and it was obvious that a lot of time and effort had gone into the entire production thus far. Robert was impressed, as was Aunt Ruby.

The second scene of the play was as intriguing as the first. Again, it ended on a cliffhanger that left the audience desperate for more. Robert was truly invested in finding out how this play would end. For the first time in a long time, he wasn't sure if good would triumph over evil as it usually did in these kinds of dramatic pieces.

He was beyond disappointed when it was announced that they would be taking an intermission.

"Honey, could you be a dear and go get me one of those bottled waters? Not too cold. And maybe some popcorn? Extra buttery, if you don't mind. With only a light sprinkling of salt," she smiled.

"No problem, Aunt Ruby. I'm a little hungry myself."

He was, in fact, famished. He hadn't eaten since lunch several hours earlier, and he felt as if he had a gaping hole where his stomach used to be.

He made his way to the parking lot, where a food truck in the shape of a hot dog beckoned him. The crowd in front of it was small, so he joined the others and patiently waited his turn. He ordered two jumbo hot dogs—one with chili and the other with onions and peppers—and a massive lemonade to wash them down. He also got Aunt Ruby's water, but since they didn't sell popcorn, he'd have to join the line in front of the concession stand inside.

The service was almost unbearably slow, and by the time he got back inside the auditorium, the fashion show was starting. He contemplated heading home, but he still had Aunt Ruby's snack. He may as well sit and eat his hot dogs. Besides, he wanted to see the end of the play. There was no law that said just because he was sitting there, he had to watch what was going on onstage.

Aunt Ruby expressed her delight over his willingness to bring her the snack. She tried to press a five-dollar bill into his hand, but he refused it, so she turned her attention to the stage.

It was like watching two trains racing towards each other on a track—he wanted to look away from the parade of teenagers, but he couldn't. His gaze kept straying back to the stage against his will.

He was horrified.

The girls on the stage were dressed almost as skimpily as streetwalkers looking for clients. Their outfits were cut up to *here* and down to *there*, their makeup gaudy and downright scary. Was *this* what Claire had been helping them to do? He could hardly believe what he was seeing. And she called herself a *Christian*?

Aunt Ruby didn't seem in the least bit perturbed, which in itself surprised Robert. Wasn't she even watching what was going on? How could she sit there and tolerate this kind of show?

"Aunt Ruby, do you have a way to get home?" He asked while hastily stuffing his half-eaten food into the paper bag.

"I'm sure Claire will take me home. Emmy had an unexpected visitor, so she decided to stay in at the last minute.

She and her friend dropped me off earlier, but I told them I'd make my way home. Are you leaving, son?"

"Yes. This is not my style." He pointed in the direction of the stage with his chin.

Aunt Ruby raised her eyebrows. "Could you stay, honey? Please? As a personal favor to me?" She placed her hand on his arm just as he was about to stand.

Though her touch was light, it was powerful. He remained, but he could feel his back teeth clenching together. He forced himself to relax. The young men on stage looked no different from some he had passed loitering in the parking lot after locking up the bookstore. In fact, he wasn't sure they weren't the same boys.

Aunt Ruby kept her hand on his arm, effectively arresting him. *All right,* he told himself, *I'll stay for a few more minutes.*

He leaned back in his seat and slowly unwrapped one of his hot dogs. He had lost his appetite—something that almost never happened—but he had to look at *something* other than the spectacle on-stage.

He bit into the chili dog and used a napkin to catch a bit of the sauce that was dribbling down his chin. He took a sip of his lemonade. It was tart, just the way he liked it. They had used fresh lemons instead of the bottled stuff that gave the lemonade an almost industrial quality. Perfect.

He kept his eyes on his food as he chewed his way through the rest of the meal. Would this cursed fashion show never end?

As soon as he'd formulated the thought, there was an eruption of applause. He turned toward the stage, and what he saw there made his blood run cold.

There, strutting her stuff on the runway all by herself, was Miss Claire Foxwood. Thankfully, she wasn't as skimpily clad as the teenagers had been much earlier. She was wearing a conservative dress and a wide smile. She walked with an air of confidence, her hand on her hip and a smile on her face. It was clear to Robert that she was completely comfortable up there. Stopping a few inches short of the runway's edge, she assumed a couple of different poses before turning and heading in the opposite direction. Halfway there, she stopped and turned again, her eyes scanning the audience and resting briefly on Robert and Aunt Ruby. Her smile faltered a bit before brightening again, and she finished the turn before heading offstage.

Robert had had enough. *Nothing*—not his desire to see the last scene of the play, not even his respect for the woman sitting beside him—could make him stay and continue witnessing this ridiculous spectacle.

He waited until he had finished packing up the remains of his meal to turn to Aunt Ruby. "I've got to go. I'll see you in church tomorrow."

He didn't give her the chance to respond before he stepped out of the row and towards the nearest exit.

☙

Claire peeked from behind the curtain and looked towards the row where Aunt Ruby and Robert had been sitting. She could see Robert making a hasty exit. She let the curtain fall back into place. What was his problem? She reflected on the outright disapproval she couldn't help but read on his face when they had called her onto the stage. She hadn't known they were going to do that; if she had, she might have worn nicer clothes. She had been enjoying her little stint on the runway until she had happened to glance in Robert Marsden's direction. The look on his face had caused her to doubt herself for a minute, and she'd almost stumbled. She hoped no one had noticed.

She couldn't figure this man out. Why had he bothered to come to the show only to leave early? He hadn't even stayed till the end of the play. She'd been surprised to see him in the audience, but she would have thought that since he had made the effort to come, he would have at least tried to stick around to the end. She suspected it had something to do with her being on-stage. But why?

What was it about this man that made her even care what he thought, anyway? She sucked her teeth in a habit she thought she had outgrown, then turned back towards the stage when she heard her name being called. What was going on out there? She peeked from behind the curtain again and wondered how she had missed the fact that all the models were back on the stage. This wasn't part of what they had practiced. She could hear the host calling her name again, so she stepped out.

"Welcome, Miss Foxwood. Please step forward."

She moved toward the front of the group amid thunderous applause from the audience.

The host spoke to the audience as the models ushered Claire forward. "As I told you at the beginning, everything we do tonight is about showing you some of the work that is being done here at the center. Miss Foxwood is one of our volunteers, and it was her predecessor that conceptualized the fashion show you just saw. The intention here tonight was to show the kind of external transformation that has been happening among some of the teenagers standing before you tonight. We thought it best to have one of the teens speak about her own experience."

Claire smiled when she saw Thea take the microphone. Thea had never been one to shy away from a challenge. In fact, Claire figured she may well have nominated herself for the task.

"Good evening, everyone. My name is Thea, and I've been coming to this center for the last nine or ten months. My mother kind of forced me to come here; she said I was getting into too much trouble at school and I needed to get focused. Remember, Momma?"

A woman close to the front stood and said, "You know that's right, baby!" The audience chuckled.

"Well, at first I didn't really like it, but then they started teaching fashion design and it didn't seem so bad anymore. When Miss Cole left, I thought about ditching the youth center, but then they told me that the lady who was going to replace her was going to be teaching about makeup and giving away free makeup kits. I decided to come see what she was about.

"Now the thing about Miss Claire is that she doesn't just teach us about makeup, although she does a great job of that. While she's showing us what to do and what not to do—which is just as important, believe me!—she also talks to us about life.

"That first day as she introduced us to primer and showed us how to choose our foundation properly, she talked about how important it is to have a firm foundation in life. It was a good talk... got me thinking, and when she handed me that makeup kit, I decided that I might come back even if she wasn't going to give me anything else.

"Then there was the time she showed us proper blending technique for eye shadows and stuff, and she spoke about balance and blending the different areas of our life together. She asked us what we were interested in—some of us liked sports, others liked reading, some just liked partying—and then she told us that no matter what we enjoyed doing, we should always mix everything together in a way that it is properly blended but also well-balanced.

"I like the way she talks to us. Even though she's an adult, she doesn't talk like she's better than us or anything. She doesn't look down on us. She just keeps stuff real. She always has. And I kept coming back, and before I knew it, I was changing a little bit.

"I mean, do you remember the outfit I was wearing when the fashion show started?" When some of the audience members shook their heads, she described it for them. "I was the one dressed in the baggy clothes with my pants sagging."

As persons among the crowd smiled and nodded their heads, she continued. "Those were my clothes. That was an actual outfit that I used to wear. I would never imagine myself in something like this, much less being the one who actually made it!" She waved her hand in front of her understated wrap dress. "I mean, I don't dress like this every day, but I understand that there's a time and a place for this, too. Miss Cole and Miss Claire taught me that. Being at this center taught me that.

"Miss Claire says that people say we shouldn't judge a book by its cover, but the truth is that people *do* judge a book by its cover. She said that we should always be mindful of our first impression on people. Now, don't get me wrong, she isn't all about people's looks. She just wants us to understand that there's got to be balance. If you wear the wrong thing to a job interview, you don't get the job because you don't understand what's expected of you. First impressions last. You can be *you* and still take other people's opinions into account.

"Even though she's a makeup artist, Miss Claire has been trying to get us to understand that no amount of makeup can cover an ugly personality. She says it's important to be beautiful inside and out. She's told each of us that there's beauty inside of us that we have to make the effort to show. We gotta let that shine through, you know? No matter what we wear on the outside, we've got to be more concerned with what's *inside*. Do you get what I'm saying?"

Scores of people in the audience smiled or nodded in agreement. Claire could feel her eyes misting over. There'd been times she'd felt like giving up; times she wondered if she should pocket more of her income instead of spending it on makeup kits she basically used to bribe the girls to keep coming to the center, but listening to Thea, she knew it was all worth it. She had helped to improve at least one teen's outlook on life, and that made it all worthwhile. In the grand scheme of things, what she was doing mattered to others, and she was grateful that God was using her to be a blessing to others. Grandy had known what she was talking about when she'd said Claire's gift would make room for her. It had opened the door to impacting the next generation, and she'd forever be grateful for that.

Right there on the stage, she began to think about other ways she could use her gift to make a positive difference in the lives of others. There was so much she could do, so many places she could offer herself and her services. There were retirement homes and women's shelters and…

The host's frantic signal for Thea to wrap it up drew Claire back to the present. She was just in time to hear the teen's closing words.

"On behalf of all the young people on the stage and those who are working behind the scenes, we want to thank Miss Claire Foxwood and all the volunteers and sponsors for the attention they've been paying to us, for the time and money they've been investing in our future. We want you all to know that we appreciate it and it won't be going to waste."

Thea found Claire and gave her a hug. She held her tightly and for once Claire felt needed, that she was in the right place at the right time. She felt loved and wanted. Amid the applause, Claire waved to the audience and quickly wiped the tear that had spilled over. The group turned and made their way off the stage, laughing and hugging.

 og

Claire could feel every muscle in her body complain as she turned the steering wheel on her way out of the parking lot at the community center. She hadn't noticed how tense she was until she'd said goodbye to Nalene, who had insisted she take Aunt Ruby home although clean-up was still underway.

"That was a resounding success, my dear. Congratulations!" Aunt Ruby beamed.

"Thank you so much. Couldn't have done it without you."

"That play... I think it was genius of them to split it into three that way. Absolutely no one wanted to leave until the very end of the event. I saw quite a number of parents with sleeping children in their arms. They probably would have left early, if not for the play."

"Well, we know the play wasn't able to keep the attention of at least *one* person." Claire felt a frown settle on her face.

"Oh?"

"You know. He was sitting right by you, Aunt Ruby."

"Oh, you mean Robert."

"I wonder what *his* problem was."

"I don't think he liked the fashion show."

"Did he even watch it?"

"Well, to be honest, I think he was paying closer attention to his dinner. I didn't even know someone could eat not one, but *two* jumbo hot dogs in a single sitting!"

Claire shrugged, which reminded her that her shoulders were super tired and tense. She needed a full body massage. If only she had the time.

"Well, he missed the best part of the show," Claire said. "I know most of the audience never saw that ending coming. When the angel and the demon descended from above the stage and did that fight scene? People were mesmerized!"

"Indeed. I really enjoyed seeing the whole thing at once. I've only seen snippets before now. The fashion show was great, too. The way you all used clothes and makeup to show the way the kids are transformed by the center... that was another genius move! And then that young lady—what was her name? Theodora?"

"Thea."

"Thea, right. She was really very articulate. Did you know she was going to speak?"

"Not at all."

"I was very moved by what she said, and I could tell others were, too. Nalene mentioned that several members of the business community spoke to her after the show. Some wanted to volunteer their time; others wanted to sponsor programs. It's fantastic!"

"Indeed! Mission accomplished." Claire was thrilled.

"I didn't get to say it to you at the time, but it was great the way you managed to calm down the lead actress."

Claire shrugged again. Ouch.

"Do you really believe what you told her?"

"Which part of it?"

"The part where you said she was fearfully and wonderfully made. You told her she was born for the role."

"Of course!" Claire turned into Aunt Ruby's driveway and stopped the car.

"But do you believe the same is true about you?"

"What do you mean?"

"I get the impression that you're still trying to figure yourself out, my dear."

Another shrug. More pain.

Aunt Ruby opened the door and set one foot outside the car. "Remember that God is no respecter of persons. If that young lady is fearfully and wonderfully made, so are you. It doesn't matter who respects you, who likes you, who finds you attractive. One person's disapproval of you is just that—one person's disapproval. God's opinion is the only one that matters, and He said that you are fearfully and wonderfully made.

"Honey, He made you beautiful in every way, and He made you for a purpose. Nothing about you surprises Him because He has never been away from you. The same chapter that tells you that you're fearfully and wonderfully made also tells you that He has every page of your life story already written down. He knows you because He made you just the way you are. You're not perfect—none of us is, but He loves you with an everlasting love, regardless of the things others might say about you. Never let anyone take that sure knowledge away from you. Good night, dear."

Before Claire could answer, Aunt Ruby stepped out of the vehicle and closed the door. As usual, she had given Claire quite a bit of food for thought.

ᘓ

Claire wondered what it was about her that had prompted Aunt Ruby to share that particular message. She thought she did a pretty good job of covering her insecurities with her bright smile and cheery personality. Apparently, she wasn't fooling this wise woman.

She supposed it was the combination of being a chubby child and being the smartest in her class. Those who didn't ridicule her for her weight would pick on her because of her high grades. Even being entered into various beauty contests hadn't completely rid her of her self-esteem issues.

When she was being completely honest with herself, she could admit that this was why she had developed an interest in makeup. It was a mask, of sorts, though not in the way people like *that man* assumed. She didn't hide behind the creams and powders; she hid behind the persona she was able to put on when she was wearing them.

On the days when she was at her lowest, she put extra effort into her appearance. She chose among her nicest clothes and she spent more time than usual on her face. Then, when she was finally ready to face the world, she walked with a level of confidence that she didn't actually feel on the inside. It was all a facade.

She had always figured that no one would be able to tell that, inside, she was still trying to convince herself that she was good enough. That she was beautiful enough. That she was strong enough. That she was smart enough. That she was *enough*. And one of the reasons *that man's* message had hurt so much was that she felt like if she stopped wearing makeup, she wouldn't have the facade to hide behind anymore. Then everyone would see all her flaws—not physical ones, but the emotional struggles she was so good at covering.

And she'd kept the mask up for years and years. Until today. For some reason, Aunt Ruby had been able to see through it all and had gotten to the root of the matter. In the silence of the car that night, Claire reflected on Aunt Ruby's words and accepted the fact that she needed to know that God loved her, and she needed to know that she was worthy of His love not because of what she wore, where she worked, what degrees she had, or anything else. He loved her because He had created her. And that was enough for Him.

And as she went through the motions that night, she heard her own voice repeating out loud, "Thank You for loving me, Lord. Thank You for loving me."

CHAPTER TWELVE

Robert tried in vain to concentrate on the rhythmical sound of his footfalls on the exercise trail. There were only a few people in the park at this time of the evening on a Friday, and he figured most of the folks who used the trail at other times were probably preparing to go out for the night. But not him. He had a rare Friday off, and it had been weeks since he'd had the time to go for a run, so once he had closed up the shop, he'd gone straight home to change into his running gear. He saw a man kneeling to adjust the collar of his dog, and he absentmindedly wondered if Claire Foxwood ever brought her dog to this park. It wasn't too far from where he'd delivered the books that day. He frowned and slowed down a little.

There she was again—smack dab in the middle of his thoughts. He hadn't interacted with the woman a lot, so why did his thoughts keep straying to her? He didn't know much about her, and wasn't impressed with what he did know, so it made no sense that he thought of her so often. Sure… she was an attractive woman, but what was she without her makeup? He was sure she would look even better if she toned down on the face-paint, maybe even cut it out altogether, so that her natural beauty could shine through.

He noticed someone walking a dog in his general direction, and as he adjusted his steps to leave some room to his left, he almost came to a complete halt. That was definitely a German Shepherd, and the woman looked suspiciously like the very person he'd just been thinking about. As she approached, he could see that it really *was* her.

She kept her eyes on the trail and he guessed that she would have moved right past him if he hadn't called her name.

"Claire?" It was as if he couldn't stop himself.

She didn't slow her gait as she held on to the dog's leash as if her life depended on it. Robert made an about turn and began to jog as slowly as he could beside her.

"Good evening, Mr. Marsden." Her stiff tone and the fact that she refused to maintain eye contact suggested that she had, in fact, seen him and had fully intended to pass without acknowledging him. Robert couldn't decide if he was annoyed or amused.

"I almost didn't recognize you dressed like that." He tilted his head towards her gray sweat pants and simple white T-shirt. Her hair was covered with a black scarf of some kind that was knotted at her nape. He wouldn't swear to it, but he didn't think she was wearing any makeup. *Will wonders never cease?*

She kept a cautious eye on Chaz, who was sniffing Robert's shoes.

He could tell she wasn't going to respond, so he decided to dive into what he wanted to say. "Aunt Ruby tells me you were at Bible study the other night." It had actually been several weeks, but who was counting?

"And?" Her tone betrayed annoyance, and Robert couldn't help but respond to it.

"Have I said something to offend you, Miss Foxwood? Or is it that I'm disturbing your walk?" He could feel his eyebrows knitting together as he asked.

Claire sighed and came to a halt. She was slow to speak, but he could sense that she was measuring her next words very carefully.

"May I ask you something, Mr. Marsden?"

He shrugged as he trotted in place, not willing to stop his run after only a couple of miles.

"That night after your Bible study, you sent me a text. Let me see if I can remember what it said. Something about being sorry I wasn't there and that you thought I could have learned something. Now that you know I actually *was* in the room, what exactly was it that you thought I should have learned?"

"Well, Miss Foxwood—" he could be just as stiff and formal as she could, "—the point I was trying to make in my presentation was that the moment a woman begins to focus on her looks to the detriment of her spirit, she's headed down a dangerous path."

"I see. And you think I'm guilty of doing that? That I'm too concerned about my looks?"

He shrugged again, "Well, if the Bedazzled shoe fits...."

He couldn't help but notice that she clenched her fists around the leash, but she remained cool as she spoke again. "And do you know me so well, then, that you are able to make that kind of judgment about me?"

"Well, Miss Foxwood, I wouldn't say I know you well, but..." he didn't want to finish his statement, but she insisted.

"Go ahead, I'd like to hear what you have to say. Enlighten me."

Since she'd asked.... "Well, Miss Foxwood," he began, "I don't see how I can think anything else. I mean, other than the first time we met and right now, every time I see you, you're wearing more makeup than the last time. Not only that, but the last time I saw you, you were strutting your stuff on a runway. And if I'm not mistaken, you were one of the people who did the makeup for the other... models. So, I really think my conclusion is a fair one."

"I see. And all of that has led you to believe that I'm more concerned about the way I look than about who I am. Let me see if I can remember the words you used in your Bible study... something like... I'm so focused on my appearance that I can make the time to look perfect while taking Chaz for a walk, but can't make it to Bible study to hear something that will edify my spirit. Was it something like that? Forgive me if my wording is off."

He couldn't miss her condescending tone. She had obviously been thinking about this for a while. He shrugged yet again. "Close enough."

"Do you go out of your way to be offensive to everyone? Or am I special?" She folded her arms and looked crossly at Robert. Chaz stood alert, as if he was aware of his owner's mood.

"Excuse me?" He wondered if he'd heard her right.

"I've wracked my brain, Mr. Marsden. I've gone over every minute of every conversation we've ever had, and the only time I remember being even a little bit rude to you was that day at your church. Clearly, my defensiveness that day made more of an impact than I thought, so please let me apologize. I'm sorry for my behavior that afternoon. I was annoyed that you had so easily forgotten me, although I obviously remembered meeting you. It was childish, and if I was rude or out of line, I'm really sorry. Now, if you don't mind, I need to go."

She stepped away from him, but Robert moved in front of her and stood with his legs wide apart and his hands on his hips, effectively blocking her path. It was amazing how attractive she was with her face free of makeup and covered in perspiration. If circumstances were different, he might be tempted to lean forward and kiss the bead of sweat from just above her top lip and then maybe he'd—

He caught himself mid-thought and tried to remember what she had just said.

As if she were aware of the direction his thoughts had taken, she retrieved a small towel that had been tucked into the waistband of her pants and mopped her face.

"Thank you for the apology, as unnecessary as it was. Exactly how have I ever been offensive to you?"

She gave a wry laugh. "I guess the word is not so much *offensive* as it is *judgmental*." She moved towards the nearby park bench, but remained standing.

"Me? Judgmental?" He was quite confused. Was he hearing right?

"You. Judgmental. Not only have you judged me—and quite incorrectly, I will tell you—but you couldn't wait to do it in public, without any concern for my feelings or whether or not your assessment of me was right. Why did you invite me? What exactly did you expect me to learn? That I was not worthy of being with someone like you? That I was somehow beneath you because I wear mascara and blush? Tell me something, Mr. Marsden, would you have used me as an example if you had known I was sitting in the room? Would you have pointed me out to the others, just in case it wasn't clear that I was the pariah you were talking about?"

Without giving him a chance to respond, she continued. "Did it ever occur to you that I got home and decided on a whim to take Chaz for a walk without stopping to remove my makeup? That perhaps I *don't* make a habit of getting perfectly made up to do stuff like this?" She lifted the leash. "And even if I did, what gives you the right to preach about it? Is that how you plan to attract people to your church when you become a pastor? By criticizing them from the pulpit and making them feel like they're unworthy of your love and respect... *and God's?*"

Robert felt his mouth fall open, and made a deliberate attempt to close it.

"Were you trying to convince me that I don't measure up to your ideal of a woman? Or maybe that I don't live up to

God's ideal? Don't you see, Mr. Marsden, that *you* are the one who is caught up in appearances?"

"Pardon me?" He was sure he was hearing things!

"You heard right! You're studying to be a pastor... a minister whose aim in life is to draw people into a closer relationship with God, yet *you* are the one who spends so much time thinking about people's outward appearance that you can't look beyond it! You never made an effort to find out who I am as a person... what the state of my soul is... whether I know the Lord. In fact, come to think of it, the first time you met me, you almost laughed at me... because of how I looked. In that moment, you decided that I wasn't even worth remembering! And that would have been fine by me, *sir*, if I didn't feel in that moment we met that something about my destiny was linked to you." She threw her hands up in the air and turned as if she was about to leave, but she clearly changed her mind, turned around and continued her verbal attack.

"You know what? I think I was right about you the first time I saw you: my destiny *is* linked to yours. You've taught me a very valuable lesson, Mr. Marsden, and without even trying. At the end of the day, *sir*, the Bible assures us that man looks at the outward appearance, while God sees our hearts. What you've taught me is that, when it comes to my walk with God and my purpose on this planet, I've got to trust my *own* convictions and not the convictions of others like yourself. Perhaps what you were destined to show me is that I've got to learn to lean on God and seek *His* approval rather than that of man. *Those* are the lessons you've reinforced for me, and I thank you for that.

"But it took a *lot* to get me here. It took tears. It took an overwhelming sense of shame and downright embarrassment that you would preach about me—and *at* me—from your position of authority. It took weeks of questioning myself, my choices, my profession… I even questioned *God* about why He made me the way He did.

"And then it took just as much time spent listening… to God, to Aunt Ruby, to myself, before I could say, 'It's a good thing Robert did that, because it helped me to see what I needed to see.'

"But I'd guess that most people won't give it weeks and months. Most people who hear judgement like that from the pulpit won't ever come back. You tell them they're not good enough for you, and that's it. You'll never have another chance to tell them the rest of the story, which is that *Christ* is good enough. That *He* is their righteousness in the very same way that He's yours, because you're human, and—pastor or not—you aren't good enough, either. Good luck keeping the pews of your future church filled, *Reverend* Marsden."

With that, she jogged away with Chaz on her heels, leaving Robert staring at her with his mouth open. Again.

Robert placed his left foot on the park bench and was about to reach for it with his right arm as he started to warm down; instead, he decided to keep running.

The nerve of that woman! He thought as he set off. He smirked and said out loud to no one in particular, "And *that*, dear friends, is why I don't need a woman in my life!"

Ω

Claire slammed the door of the house with such anger that the picture frame on the nearby wall shook. She couldn't remember a time she'd been so upset. She wasn't usually the confrontational type. She always avoided arguments like the proverbial plague, and on countless occasions had given up her rights rather than stand up for them. She couldn't figure out what it was about that... *that man* that made her feel like she needed to let him have it.

She had seen him before he'd seen her, and her heart had started pounding in a way that hadn't happened in years. Her palms had moistened from something other than mere sweat, and she'd had to take several deep breaths to calm herself. It was annoying that she still found that... *that man* attractive. The whole situation reminded her of Lamont Jefferson, the boy she'd had a crush on way back in high school. She'd still liked him even after he let her know that dating a chubby girl like her would never happen, not even if she were the last person on the face of the planet. She'd been disappointed to learn that he was a near-sighted bigot. Be that as it may, it hadn't immediately caused her attraction to the football player to evaporate, as much as she wished it had. It had taken months to get over him. That... *that man* had a way of making her feel the same way she'd felt then. She was even more annoyed with herself now. She was a grown woman, after all; teenage crushes ought to be a thing of the past.

Since it would have been too obvious if she'd turned around and run off screaming in the opposite direction, she'd lowered her head and tried to move past him without him noticing her and her dog. It had failed. And miserably.

If only he hadn't said her name. If only her body hadn't melted at the sound of his voice.

She was still angry when she wrenched open the pantry door and reached for a bottle of water from the shelf. Chaz trotted into the kitchen and looked at her expectantly, but she ignored him. He could have a treat later.

Stomping into the living room, she sank into the rocking recliner, which lurched backwards. The unanticipated movement caused her to splash water all over herself, the recliner and the floor, and she felt herself becoming even more upset.

What was it about that... *that man* that allowed him to get to her the way he had? Okay, so he was attractive, but she saw attractive men every day. He was ambitious, but there were similar men all around. He apparently shared her love of reading, but so what? So did one of the other volunteers at the community center, a widowed man of no less than sixty-five who was always inviting her out to lunch.

She sighed. She knew exactly what it was.

She was disappointed.

That day she'd come to the screen door and made eye contact with Robert Marsden, she had felt an irrevocable shift in her spirit. She'd re-examined the situation several times since then, and that's the only way she could really describe it. She had looked at him and she had known that he would be an important part of her life. She groaned loudly as she realized that she had said as much to him in her monologue earlier.

She'd never have admitted it to anyone, but despite what she'd said to him earlier, she had actually been harboring some kind of misplaced hope that he was the man God had designed for her. To find out that not only was he *not* attracted to her, but that he'd also judged her and found her lacking without even making an effort to get to know her... well, it hurt like heck.

She didn't know why, but she could see herself with *that man*—a less judgmental version, of course—for the rest of her life. Cheering him on as he crossed the stage at graduation. Praying him through his first sermon as a pastor. Standing beside him on-stage. Shaking hands with people after church. Laying in his arms after a hard day. Caressing him and loving him in every way.

And it wasn't like she'd ever wanted to be a minister's wife. In fact, she'd always felt sorry for the wives of the pastors in the churches she'd attended. They always seemed to be pulled in a thousand different directions as they supported their husband in his ministry. She'd often wondered if those women didn't have independent ministries of their own. What was it about all of them that made them nurturers, Sunday School teachers, choir directors, church secretaries and more? Was there some kind of course at the seminary that taught a woman how to stand a few feet behind her man?

She'd always wondered these things, and had never aspired to fit into that mold. She just wanted to reach people in her own way. If that meant teaching teenage girls how to apply makeup that wouldn't cause them to be a spectacle among their peers, then she was satisfied with that. If it involved praying with young brides while she applied their bridal makeup on their wedding day, then that was what she would do. If it meant going into retirement homes and helping the residents feel young again for a few hours, then where could she sign up?

Now this man had come along and made her doubt herself. She was glad that was over. But it still hurt that he didn't like her... not even a little bit. She needed to remind herself who she was in God's sight. She made up her mind to post a reminder on her fridge so she would see it often. She knew exactly what she would write: Claire Foxwood, you are God's design, and you are fearfully and wonderfully made!

She trotted into the kitchen for a handful of paper towels to mop up the water she'd spilled earlier and smiled.

She may not have approached Robert the way she usually would have, but she was pretty sure she'd gotten his attention about his judgmental attitude. Good! She hoped she'd given him something to think about. In a roundabout way, God had used Robert to reach Claire and teach her things about herself that she needed to know; maybe God was using her to reach him, too.

CHAPTER THIRTEEN

From his position on the floor of the bookstore, Robert unpacked items from the box of used books one at a time and handed them to Aunt Ruby, who would enter the relevant information into the computer. Robert was quite proud of her. She had never operated a computer before working at the store, but now she was fairly competent at what he needed her to do. He didn't think she was ready to send instant messages or emails just yet, but maybe in time....

Aunt Ruby chuckled when he handed her a title he could tell was considerably old, based on its cover.

"What's so funny?" He was curious.

"This book. It was one of my husband's favorites. He would read it over and over, but I never was able to get past the first chapter without my eyes glazing over." She shook her head as she smiled. "Maybe I should buy it and make another attempt."

Robert shrugged. He would have offered to give it to her, but he knew she wouldn't take it. She was forever telling him that he would never turn a consistent profit if he kept giving away the merchandise.

"You two were pretty happy together, huh?"

"We were, for the time we had, which wasn't much."

Robert knew Howard Crawford had passed away within a few years of getting married to Aunt Ruby. "Would you ever consider getting married again, Aunt Ruby?"

"Why? Are you proposing?" She gave him a cheeky grin.

He raised his arms defensively. "Who? Me? No offense, Aunt Ruby, but I don't think that road is for me."

"What road? Marriage?"

He nodded solemnly.

"Why not? It's an honorable institution created by God."

"For sure, but like Saint Paul said, it's not for everybody."

"True, but don't write it off. It can be a beautiful thing. Out of curiosity, why are you so dead set against it? Have you had your heart broken?"

Robert flashed her a grin. "Not since Eloise Edwardson broke up with me two nights before senior prom."

Arched eyebrows betrayed her surprise. "Do you mean to tell me that a handsome man like you hasn't had a date in... what's it been... more than ten years?"

It was his turn to chuckle. "Oh, I've been on lots of dates since high school! I've even been in a few semi-serious relationships, but my heart just hasn't gotten into the mix. They always like me more than I liked them."

"So you haven't seen any nice, Christian girls that catch your attention enough to consider the long term?"

Robert felt his smile fade away as an unbidden image of Claire Foxwood popped into his mind's eye. "To be honest, Aunt Ruby, the Christian women I've dated... well... they've always been in some kind of rush to the altar, but none of them have tempted me to go there with them."

"Really?" Aunt Ruby seemed thoughtful.

"Really." He confirmed with a sharp nod.

"What about Claire Foxwood?"

Robert couldn't hide his grimace.

"What?" Aunt Ruby hadn't missed it.

"Not my type."

"And what type would that be? She's saved. She's smart. She's articulate. She has her own business. She serves her community with the work she's doing over at the community center. And if all that wasn't enough to make you happy, she's pretty, to boot."

"How pretty she is... that's a matter of opinion, Aunt Ruby." Even as he heard himself say the words, he knew he was not being completely truthful. He thought back to their last meeting, when he had seen her in the park... the time when all she had been wearing on her face was hard-earned sweat. The truth was, she was *fine*... with or without makeup.

"Ahhh... now we come to the crux of the matter. You don't find her attractive?"

He shrugged. "It doesn't matter if I do or don't. I don't like her."

"I see. Have you ever had a conversation with her? I mean, just the two of you?"

"Yes."

"And?"

"She was rude and offensive."

"Claire?" Aunt Ruby's tone exuded disbelief.

"The one and the same."

"I find it hard to believe she would just walk up to you and say something rude or offensive. She must have been provoked."

"Well, provoked or not, she was completely off-base. Can you imagine she had the nerve to accuse me of being judgmental! A woman like *her*."

Aunt Ruby put down the book she had been perusing and looked over her glasses at Robert.

"And did she say why she thought that?"

Robert shrugged from his place on the floor. "Something about me judging her because of her looks. Something about me being the one who was overly concerned with outward appearances. I find it ridiculous, really. I mean, if I were overly concerned about the way people look, why would I have taught a Bible study about beauty beginning on the inside? I mean, *come on!*" He got to his feet and leaned his hip against the counter, his arms crossed in front of him.

"Actually, son…"

Robert knew that Aunt Ruby only called him 'son' when she was preparing to impart what she thought was indispensable wisdom. He sighed inwardly. He didn't really want to be preached to right now.

"Son, you left the fundraiser a bit abruptly the other night. May I ask why?"

"I didn't want to be there anymore."

"I don't believe you for a minute. You wanted to see the end of that play just like everyone else."

"Okay, you got me there. Truth is, I was annoyed because I saw Claire backstage before the show started. She was applying makeup to those teenage girls' faces, and I didn't like that. Then on top of that, she actually came out on the stage and modeled. A Christian woman! Modeling!" He could feel himself getting upset again. "And she has the nerve to say *I'm* the one who's caught up with looks!"

Aunt Ruby's tone was measured. "So when you got up, you left right away?"

"Yes."

"Well, then, you missed the best part. Did you even notice what was going on while you were there? Did you see that when those kids came out they were wearing their own clothes—the clothes they used to wear before coming to the center? Did you see the way their clothes and makeup changed as the fashion show progressed? You probably didn't even notice that. You were too busy being upset. I saw the way you were studying those hot dogs like you were prepping for one of your exams.

"Did it ever occur to you, my dear Robert, that God might actually be using Claire's makeup artistry to reach people for Him that you and I could never reach?"

Robert wrinkled his brow. "Meaning?"

"Claire offers free makeup lessons and kits to the girls at the center. The makeup draws them in. And then as she's doing what she does, she helps them to understand the importance of developing as holistic individuals and not just pretty young things."

Robert was sure Aunt Ruby thought her use of the eighties term was quite up-to-date. He couldn't help but scoff. "Oh, is that what she told you?"

"No. That's what one of the girls told the audience on Saturday night. Had you stuck around, you'd have heard it yourself.

"According to the young lady—I forgot her name but I think it starts with a 'T'—Claire helps them to develop confidence in themselves as valuable human beings, created in God's image to do His will, and not just as sex objects who have nothing to offer but their bodies. She's helping them build their self-confidence, and at the same time she's equipping them with a marketable skill. On top of that, she's teaching them that they are fearfully and wonderfully made. She is doing God's work over at that center, Robert. *God's work.*"

Robert was surprised.

"If you'd come out of your little cocoon long enough to see why she was onstage, you'd have learned all about the difference Claire makes in the lives of these young ladies. She may use the makeup as a tool, but she is channeling God's word while she does it. And while her methods may be very different from yours or mine, we have to admit that she has a platform you and I might never have. Those girls may never come into this store because those who *do* read might not have the money to buy the kinds of books that we sell. They may never darken the doorsteps of a church because churches are full of 'church people.' They're afraid they won't be dressed right; that the members of the church are going to judge them based on their clothes and their makeup and their hair and their shoes. But they'll sit through a session on how to dress for a job interview if they know they're going to get a free makeup kit at the end of it." Aunt Ruby took her glasses off and set them on the counter. She gazed so deeply into Robert's eyes that he wanted to look away. It was as if she was reading his thoughts.

"When we surrender to God, Robert, we are asking Him to use us where we are. *That* is what Claire is doing. Her gift in makeup artistry is making room for her. Like it says in Ephesians two, Claire Foxwood is God's handiwork, created in Christ for the works that God Himself prepared in advance for *her* to do. That's *her* work, and it's very different from yours or mine. And you have no right to dismiss her outright because she doesn't look the way you want her to look.

"The truth is, my son, any minister would be beyond fortunate to have a woman like Claire beside him. But *you* have already decided that you won't be that man, because in writing her off, you've already written *yourself* off because of the way she looks. You're blocking your own blessing, and you're too blind and stubborn to see it. And don't tell me you don't think she's gorgeous, because I saw the way you looked at her at that potluck. I saw that look in your eyes when she stepped out onto that stage at the fundraiser. And don't tell me I'm wrong, because if you weren't attracted to her... if you didn't *feel* something for her, there's no way you'd have been so upset about her participating in the show in the first place. So you can keep denying it to yourself, but don't even think about starting that with me."

Robert wasn't sure how to respond, so he said nothing for several minutes. Aunt Ruby had certainly given him a lot to think about. And some stuff to pray about, too. He struggled to remember what they had been talking about before Claire Foxwood's name had come up. *Oh. Marriage. That was it*, he said to himself. A much safer topic than the one they'd just been discussing. Much safer.

"You might have a point there, Aunt Ruby, but it's something I'll have to think about. You know us men, right? We need time to process stuff. You can't lay all of that on me and expect me to answer you right away.

"But back to our earlier discussion about marriage. I guess the truth is that marriage has never been high on my list of priorities. I mean, I have the store and I have my studies. Where would I find time for a relationship? Besides, I guess God hasn't given me a sign that marriage is His will for my life."

Aunt Ruby set her glasses back on her face and looked up with a mischievous grin on her face. "Oh, you want a sign? Is that all? A sign?" She looked skyward and spoke in an exaggerated voice, "Oh, Lord, I beseech Thee—don't let this good Christian boy and his exceptional genes go to waste. If the boy wants a sign, Lord, then please give the boy a sign sooner, rather than later! Thank You in advance, Lord, because I know the sign is already on its way. Amen!"

Almost before she'd finished speaking, there was a loud crash followed by a commotion across the street from the bookstore. They both stopped what they were doing and headed towards the big glass window at the front of the store. From what Robert could tell, workers installing a new sign onto a shop front across the street had fumbled, causing it to fall to the ground. Robert almost choked when he read the logo on the truck parked right in front of the building. His mouth fell open. *What the—?*

The logo on the side of the truck said *Foxwood's Signage. Looking for a sign? Foxwood's the one.*

There was an audible snap when Robert forcefully closed his mouth, but he pretended he didn't hear Aunt Ruby's rather loud squeal as she read the sign herself.

&#x03 memory;

He would never have admitted it to a soul, but the future Reverend Robert Marsden was thrilled that he was super busy for the next few days. Usually, he'd have been a little flustered having to run the business, study for finals and prepare for presentations, but this time around, he was relieved. He was glad he had so much on his mind; he was glad that at nights he had no choice but to fall into bed and into a deep, dreamless sleep; he was glad he didn't have the time to reflect on what Aunt Ruby had told him. He was glad.

But the busy cycle came to an end, and Robert was faced with the task of trying to distill whatever it was that God was trying to teach him in this period. He hadn't been able to run for the last week, so he donned his sweats and headed for the park. He didn't expect to run into... anyone. He didn't want to analyze why he was going to the park on the same day of the week and at roughly the same time as he'd bumped into Claire Foxwood the last time he'd seen her. Had it only been a few weeks ago? It seemed like much longer.

For the first time since his discussion with Aunt Ruby, he allowed himself to actually concentrate on the situation at hand. He decided to start with the sign and work his way backward.

Was it mere coincidence that as soon as Aunt Ruby had prayed for a sign, an actual *sign* had appeared right in front of him? He played the end of the conversation over in his mind. He had told Aunt Ruby that he didn't know if he was supposed to get married, that God hadn't given him a sign about that. Then she'd prayed that God would deliver one, and within a minute, a literal sign had appeared in front of his eyes. *Looking for a sign? Foxwood's the one.*

And though he hadn't admitted it to himself at the time, he'd felt a very unfamiliar inkling in his spirit that the whole commotion outside had somehow been orchestrated just for him.

Which led him to something Claire had mentioned the last time they'd seen each other in this very park—something he hadn't allowed himself to process until this very minute. She had said that the first time she'd seen him, she had felt in her spirit that her destiny was somehow linked to his. Had she gotten some kind of *sign* the first time they'd met all those months ago? He winced. Why would God do this? Why would God choose two people who were so obviously *not* suited for each other and link them together?

God clearly had some kind of sense of humor! The woman was infuriating. He couldn't imagine spending the rest of his life fighting for space at the bathroom vanity where she would no doubt lay out her makeup application arsenal. He could just see himself trying to find his own things among all the stuff she undoubtedly used on her face. His imagination began to run wild as he made his way across the park.

There was a double vanity with all sorts of makeup paraphernalia strewn across both sides. He was standing there in a white T-shirt and a pair of boxers with his hands on his hips, a white gold wedding band clearly visible in the mirror. He couldn't name any of his wife's weapons, but they were all over the place. All he needed was a disposable razor. He felt helpless. He didn't even know where to begin looking for one.

A familiar voice sounded from somewhere close to the bathroom door. "What's the matter, honey?"

He shrugged without turning around. "Razor?"

He watched in the mirror as Claire approached the vanity, diamonds and white gold glistening from her left hand. In his mind, she was wearing flannel pajama pants and an oversized white T-shirt that was probably his. Her hair was swept back away from her face with some kind of hairband. He expected her face to be makeup free — this was his vision, after all! — but he could tell she had done something to her eyelashes and there was definitely something making her cheeks glow. Her lips looked plump and enticing, and as she reached around him to open the drawer right beside him, he detected the slightest fragrance of strawberries. She was wearing his favorite lip gloss again. He forgot why he had even come into the bathroom in the first place. Stubbly chin or not, he reached for her and playfully dipped her like a ballroom dancer. He smiled gleefully and pressed his lips against hers. Her mouth parted slightly, allowing him to explore her even further.

Robert shook his head briskly and came back to the present before his imagination went too far. Instead, he tried to concentrate on his running. *Left, right, left, right, left, right...*

It didn't work.

What was it Aunt Ruby had said? That Claire's gift was making room for her? What gift? Makeup artistry? Surely, that wasn't a gift God gave people! In his mind, he flipped pages in his well-used Bible until he came to the fourth book of Ephesians. What did it say in verse eleven? Something about Christ gifting some to be apostles, prophets, evangelists, pastors and teachers? And what about First Corinthians 12:28, where reference was made to apostles, prophets, teachers, healers, helpers, guides and those who spoke in tongues? He hadn't managed to memorize his Bible from cover to cover, but he was pretty sure there wasn't any mention of the gift of making women appear different than they really were. There was no gift of makeup artistry!

His mind seemed determine to wander, though, and soon he began to consider the people in his life and what gifts they may have been given. He believed that he was anointed to be a pastor and a teacher. Running the bookstore wasn't his gift; it was something that allowed him to share his love of reading with others and something he hoped would pay the bills for a few years until he was settled in his ministry. By being very selective about his catalog and charitable with his earnings, he tried to use it to reach people for Christ, but it wasn't really his calling.

But what about Aunt Ruby? What was her gift? She often told him that she had wanted to be a teacher like her sister Emmy, but she had realized from a short stint teaching Sunday School that she didn't have the right skills to make teaching work. She was warm and friendly, but she couldn't take a lesson and fashion it in such a way as to make others 'get it.' They would enjoy the class, but at the end of it, the students were more likely to remember the examples she had shared with them than the underlying theme of the class. She always joked about being glad their church didn't do Sunday School exams, because the students would probably have failed miserably. Warmth and friendliness could only go *so far* in the classroom. Teaching was certainly *not* her gift. Instead, she had been a health inspector by profession, and now she helped him out in the bookstore so he could have the time to go to seminary. She was definitely one of God's gifts to the future Reverend Robert Marsden!

He knew from the few times they were in the shop together that there were customers who only came in when she was there. They would hang around for hours sometimes, just talking to her. He could see the change in them—even the teenagers that came in—after spending time in her presence. If there were gifts to the body of Christ that were not mentioned specifically in the Bible, then maybe hers was the ability to listen and share insightful messages that made people think. Even when they didn't want to.

Robert thought about his own parents. His father sang and directed the church choir on Sundays, but he was a mail carrier during the week. His pleasant disposition brought a smile to the face of everyone on his route, and he invited so many of them to church that their pastor often joked that Simon Marsden was personally responsible for the size of the membership.

His mother was a housewife, but she was part of the church's prayer circle. He couldn't count the times he'd gone home to find his mother on the phone praying with some church member who was going through challenging times.

Robert continued to pound the pavement as he made lap after lap on the jogging trail. But then something strange began to happen. He thought about his sister, Georgina, who for years had been a housewife with a passion for scrapbooking before she began selling handmade craft items. She'd eventually opened her own small business and had been able to hire someone to help her. The way she could turn abstract scraps of paper or wood into three-dimensional pieces that spoke of God's glory... well, suffice it to say that Robert knew his sister's hands were probably more gifted than his mouth could ever be.

Countless other examples came to mind, and he knew the Holy Spirit was pouring something into him that he had never considered before. How could he have missed the fact that people were gifted in ways that had nothing to do with serving in the church sanctuary? Aunt Emmy's teaching. His mother's praying. His father's smile. Aunt Ruby's wisdom. His friend Daniel's research. He could see clearly now that all these capacities were gifts that could be used to honor God, to bring Him glory, and to bring lost sheep into the fold. Didn't the Bible say somewhere in the book of James that every good and perfect gift was from above? Why should Claire Foxwood's gift be any different, especially since—if what Aunt Ruby had said was true—she was already using it to impact the lives of young girls in a positive way? Whose life was *he* impacting?

He slowed to a jog. He thought about the number of true friends he had—the number of people he shared the love of God with, outside the pulpit. It was only a few. Was it his judgmental spirit that kept people from getting close to him? Is this what kept Claire away?

Maybe there was a smidgen of truth to how she felt.

He took a seat on a nearby bench and realized that, besides his friend Daniel, Aunt Ruby and Aunt Emmy, there were few people in his life that he could open up to. When he had gotten the chance to get to know Claire, he'd ceremoniously dismissed her and written her off without so much as a second thought. She was right. It was *he* who had judged her based on her looks and the fact that she wore makeup.

He remembered how insulted he had felt when that police officer had assumed he was flirting with her. He'd wanted to defend himself. He'd wanted to call her out on how wrong she was in jumping to conclusions about him based on very little information. Claire must have felt the same way.

Robert closed his eyes and imagined how she must have felt as he'd actually preached a sermon about her—*while she was sitting in the room.* He felt ashamed of himself. *How do I make this right?* Robert wondered.

CHAPTER FOURTEEN

Claire popped a worship album into her portable CD player and settled into her beloved rocking recliner. The piece of furniture had cost a pretty penny when she'd bought it several years earlier, but it had been worth every cent. She pulled the lever to raise the foot rest and settled in.

It had been a long time since she'd had a Saturday afternoon to herself. Ever since she'd started giving of her time and energy at the community center, she had been super busy. The only reason she could relax this afternoon was the fact that the kids had gone on a field trip with some of the other volunteers. She'd been invited to accompany them, of course, but she needed the break. Between the store and the center, as well as the other projects she'd taken on recently, she'd been going non-stop for weeks and weeks, and she needed this time to rejuvenate.

Knowing she would have some time to read today, she'd decided to stop at Notes in the Margin the day before, and on her way out the door, Aunt Ruby had handed her a fairly heavy gift bag.

"I saw this and thought of you, honey," she had said. When Claire moved to open the bag, Aunt Ruby added, "Wait till you get home. I really want you to meditate on the words for a while."

Claire, though surprised, had complied, but had forgotten about it when she got home the previous evening. She reached into the gift bag, and among sheets of tissue paper, she found a three-dimensional wall plaque with a calligraphy scripture at its center. As she read the words, they settled in her spirit like no other scripture had ever done. For some reason, Aunt Ruby had chosen the words of James 1:17, which simply said, "Every good gift and every perfect gift is from above and comes down from the Father of lights, with whom is no change or shadow of turning."

She barely noticed the craftsmanship as she ran her fingers over the textured wooden plaque.

"Every good gift and every perfect gift is from above..." it said. What was Aunt Ruby trying to tell her? She thought back to the evening of the fundraiser when Aunt Ruby had been watching her apply makeup to the face of one of the teenage models.

"I had no idea it took all of those steps to do makeup properly," Aunt Ruby admitted. "I tend to stick with my eyebrow pencil and lipstick, to be honest. Maybe a little powder to take the sheen off the face, you know."

Claire smiled. "My mother doesn't even wear that much."

"No? So how come you got interested in makeup?" Aunt Ruby wanted to know.

"My grandmother was a huge fan. She would get all made up, and suddenly she'd have more of a pep in her step. She'd hold her head higher when her hair was done. She said she liked to make a good impression. I was just fascinated by the transformation. She had a look for every occasion—understated for trips to the store, classic for church, and more dramatic for when my grandpa took her dancing. The moment she showed me how to apply blush to the apples of my cheeks, I was completely hooked! My mother still doesn't understand, but she's glad I got certified and opened my own store. Like she says, 'If you're gonna do somethin', do it right!'"

"She's right about that. You certainly are gifted!"

"Oh, I don't know about that, Aunt Ruby. It's not like I'm a neurosurgeon or anything."

"God doesn't make mistakes, you know. He made you just the way you are, and He knows everything about You. All of us have improvements we can make, but even so, the best thing we can do is lay ourselves at His feet and say, 'Use me for Your glory, Lord.' It seems to me that you've done that. After all, look at what you're doing."

Claire finished with the model she'd been working with and turned to her next 'client.' The young lady who sat in the chair was literally shaking.

"What's wrong?"

"I'm soooo nervous! I've never acted in a play before! Now they've given me the lead! They must be crazy. I can't do this!"

"Calm down, honey," Claire had soothed her. She moved behind the girl and began to give her a quick shoulder rub. "You've got this. I've watched you for the past few weeks. You're the first one to get to rehearsal and the last one to leave. You know your lines inside and out, backwards and forwards. You sing like an angel and your speaking voice is strong and clear. You are fearfully and wonderfully made, and this role was made for you. You've got this. Now, take some deep breaths."

The young lady did as she was told, gulping down the air like she'd been underwater for too long.

"Slowly. In through the nose; hold it for a few seconds; out through the mouth. Now that you've stopped shaking so much, I'm going to apply some false eyelashes."

"Wh-why?"

"Well, honey, when you're on-stage, the audience can hardly see your facial features, so we have to amp them up a bit so they can be seen by everyone. You have these gorgeous eyes, so big and expressive, so we want to bring a little attention to them...."

By the time she was finished, the lead actress had calmed down. She gave Aunt Ruby and Claire a quick hug and stepped away.

"That's exactly what I'm talking about, Claire. Not only do you have gifted hands, but you can make people feel better from the inside out. That young lady is more confident than when she sat in this chair, and not everyone can do that with blush and lipstick."

She looked towards the door and suddenly said, "Oh, I think I see my guest!" before making a quick exit, leaving Claire and Mitzie to transform the rest of the cast.

Claire looked at the piece of art again. "Every good gift and every perfect gift is from above…."

"Is this what You've been trying to show me, Lord? That I shouldn't ignore my gifts just because they're not like other people's gifts? I know Your Word says my gifts will make room for me. Is that why these new opportunities are coming my way? Have my gifts been making room for me, Lord? Is that why they welcomed me, first at the community center, and now at the nursing home. with the monthly visits Mitzie and I have committed to? Is that why business has been booming lately, especially since I felt like I needed to change the name from Outside-In to Inside-Out? Are those open doors Your way of confirming that this gifting I have is indeed from You, and not of the devil, as has been implied?"

She sat quietly and waited to see if the Lord would speak to her the way He spoke to Aunt Ruby. In the silence, she began to experience something she could only describe as complete and utter peace. It was as if a feeling of joy had bloomed on the inside of her chest and was spreading outward.

Claire recognized the feeling as the exact opposite of the burden she had sensed and felt when she had met Nalene Betancourt at the bookstore and later at her own store. She hadn't even noticed that the burden had lifted when she had agreed to teach the girls.

Was this what Saint Paul was talking about when he had mentioned "the peace that passes all understanding"? It certainly felt like it. In this very moment, she understood that her ability to make people feel better about themselves was a gift that God Himself had chosen—in His infinite wisdom—to bestow on her. Her use of makeup sessions to spread God's love was another.

She noticed that the song coming from her CD player was one of her favorites, and she began to sing in a voice she didn't want her neighbors to hear, but that she knew the Lord would appreciate. She became acutely aware of her sinful nature, and that the only claim she could ever have to righteousness was through Christ alone. As she surrendered to the feeling, she felt unworthy of reclining in the presence of God, so she dropped the foot rest and slid out of the recliner and down to the floor. She lay flat, her forehead, her nose, and even her lips touching the laminate.

She couldn't speak, but she knew her mind was crying out to the Lord who had come to visit her in her living room. "Thank You for speaking to me, Lord. Please continue to use me for Your glory. I consecrate myself and these gifts for Your service and dedicate all that I am to You. Use me in any way You see fit. I will humbly go where You want me to go and do what You want me to do."

೮೩

She stayed there in the presence of God until she found herself waking up. She hadn't even noticed that she'd fallen asleep on the floor. With great effort, she sat back on her heels, her knees still in contact with the floor. With the back of her hand, she wiped some drool that had drained out of her mouth and found its way to the vicinity of her chin during her nap. *Eww!*

The CD had started skipping during the very last song, so she maneuvered herself into a standing position and pressed the stop button. She stretched. She'd actually been lying on the ground for over an hour. She didn't know the point at which worship had given way to rest, but she felt amazing. She bent to retrieve the wall plaque from where it had fallen on the floor, and for the first time she noticed how exquisite it was.

It was made from a rustic piece of wood, and someone had used a very fine instrument to carve the words into its surface. It must have taken forever! She turned it over to see who had made it. The logo said "Made exclusively for you by Georgina Marsden Baker." Had Aunt Ruby ordered a custom-made gift?

Marsden. Now there was a name that hadn't come to her mind for a while.

It had taken a couple of months, but Claire Foxwood felt like she was *finally* over Robert Marsden. She was *finally* able to go through an entire day without thinking about him. She had come to realize that her destiny really *was* tied to his, but not in the way she had expected and probably even hoped. His sojourn in her life had been brief and had never really developed beyond a few conversations, but she felt that God had used him to boost her self-confidence and to give her a clearer picture of how He wanted to use her.

Through a series of events and conversations starting with his Bible study, Claire had embarked on a journey of self-discovery even as she made a conscious effort to understand more about who God was and how He operated.

Robert had probably hoped that his message would have convicted her in certain areas, but that had not happened the way he may have expected. What Claire experienced was the Lord's conviction in other areas of her life.

Ironically, her conviction was based on the same scriptures that Robert had tried to use against her. The more she read the passages from First Peter chapter three and First Timothy chapter two, the more she realized that although her heart was in the right place, she did not have the gentle, quiet spirit of which Peter had written nor the submissive nature Paul had advocated to Timothy.

As she examined herself, she came to understand that there were many aspects of her personality that left a lot to be desired. She suspected she would be praying for a submissive spirit for the rest of her life, but she also knew there were many other areas in which she felt short. She tended to be abrupt with others. She was easily offended—thin-skinned, her mother used to call her—and tended to overcompensate by being offensive. She was sometimes dismissive of the feelings of others and liked to talk about herself a bit too much. She had begun to feel as if there was nothing good inside of her except the fact that she had invited Jesus into her heart a year earlier.

She'd started crying out to God for a gentle, quiet spirit that would be less offensive and more welcoming to others. She had also asked that the Lord would help her to submit to those in a position of authority over her, including—maybe even *especially*—her future husband.

Morning after morning had found her on her knees in repentance over her mean ways. She had stopped kidding herself. She was far from perfect. She knew it and the Holy Spirit knew it. At least she was willing to acknowledge where she was going wrong—which was more, she figured, than Robert Marsden.

But she was trying hard not to judge him. He had wounded her deeply with his condemnation of her, but she had prayed for the Lord to help her to forgive him so that she would no longer hold his words against him. She hadn't seen him since that evening at the park, but she hoped that if she were to bump into him somewhere, she would be able to speak to him without bitterness.

She wasn't in a hurry for any of that to happen.

CHAPTER FIFTEEN

Robert took several deep breaths before he pushed the door and entered the store. It was his first time in a makeup store, and he wasn't sure what to expect... only that he would feel out of place.

It had been several weeks since what he had come to consider 'The Sign Incident' and even longer since he'd seen Claire. He had hoped to run into her somewhere—maybe the bookstore or the park—but it hadn't happened thus far, and he really wanted to speak with her. He'd eventually decided to take the bull by the horns and come to the place where he was sure to find her—her job.

The store was by no means cluttered, but he was still overwhelmed by the sheer volume of products on display. The walls showed pictures of various facial features—eyes, lips, cheeks—and he guessed that below the pictures were products designed to enhance those features.

The display units were black and set against horizontal black and white wallpaper stripes. In the middle of the store was a counter with a pair of contemporary bar stools in front of it and a cash register to one side. He guessed that must be where makeovers and such were done.

He didn't recognize the woman who was talking with a customer over by the section of the store dedicated to cheeks. She was young and had her hair wrapped in a black turban. She smiled in his direction and held up one finger, indicating that he should wait. He browsed the store while she continued attending to the needs of her client.

Robert felt awkward . As he walked around the store, he was surprised to see a framed quotation among the pictures on the walls. The words were printed in crisp white against a red background and encased in a black frame mounted on an otherwise bare section of wall that separated two sets of display units.

The quotation was simple:

Beauty is not in the face; beauty is a light in the heart.
— *Kahlil Gibran*

Robert felt his brow wrinkle. *Well*, he said to himself, *that was certainly unexpected in a store like this!* He kept walking and stopped again when he came to another frame.

Outer beauty attracts, but inner beauty captivates.
— *Kate Angell*

His curiosity piqued, he moved along the wall until he found another frame.

Beauty isn't about having a pretty face. It is about having a pretty mind, a pretty heart, and most importantly, a beautiful soul.

— *Anonymous*

He'd never been in a makeup store until today, but he certainly didn't expect to see quotations about inner beauty all over the place. Wasn't the whole store—the whole industry—dedicated to external beauty? On the left side of the exit door, he read:

Take care of your inner, spiritual beauty. That will reflect in your face.

— *Dolores Del Rio*

To the right of the door was yet another, proclaiming that:

> *Inner beauty radiates from within, and there's nothing more beautiful than when a woman feels beautiful on the inside.*
> — Erin Heatherton

He moved towards the center of the store, and there on the counter was another frame, the highlighted words very familiar to him. He reached for the frame and read the quotation, although he didn't really need to. He had already memorized it.

> *Your beauty should not come from outward adornment.... Rather, it should be that of your inner self, the unfading beauty of a gentle and quiet spirit, which is of great worth in God's sight.*
> — 1 Peter 3:3-4 (NKJV)

He was surprised to hear a voice coming from right beside him. He hadn't even noticed that the young lady with the turban was standing next to him.

"Good afternoon. May I help you?"

He still had the frame in his hand when he turned to greet her. "Hello there." Her eyes were the darkest he had ever seen... maybe even black. He had to make an effort not to raise his eyebrows.

"Nice, isn't it?" She smiled as she looked in the direction of the frame.

Robert gently returned it to its spot behind the register.

"Yes. Kind of... odd, wouldn't you say?"

"Whaddya mean? In a makeup store?"

Robert guessed she was not much more than twenty years old. The lipstick she wore was very dark against her fair skin, and her blue nose ring sparkled under the lights. Her eyes were heavily lined in black and topped with various shades of metallic shadows. Robert found himself wanting to look at anything but her black eyes, but he didn't want to stare at her mouth in case she thought he was some kind of pervert. He settled for her nose bridge.

She grinned. "We're experimenting with the gothic look today. Don't worry about it. I promise I don't look like this every day!"

"Oh..." he wasn't sure how to respond. He racked his brain to remember what he had wanted to ask her about. When it came to him, he pointed at the scripture on the counter.

"Yeah. It's kind of out of place, isn't it? I mean, aren't you more or less selling *outer* beauty here? Isn't that a conflict of interest?"

"You could look at it that way, but we don't."

"How so?" He leaned against the counter and propped his elbow beside the frame.

"Well, we *do* sell products that enhance physical beauty. But we also want our clients to know that God don't like ugly, if you know what I mean."

"I'm not sure I do."

The young woman, whose name tag identified her as Mitzie, went to stand behind the cash register. "We may be selling makeup, sir, but at the end of the day, the makeup comes off. In fact, we sell products for that, too!" She grinned before becoming serious again. "Makeup is great, but it's only skin-deep. Women use it to give the right impression; to present ourselves as professionals; to dress up for a special occasion; to add a little variety to our lives. But that gets us the attention of mankind. We here at Inside-Out... the owner and I... we're believers, and we believe that God looks beyond all that. He sees the heart. The way we look is not as important to Him as the way we *are*... our attitude... our actions... whether we're bringing Him glory. Do you see what I'm saying?"

He nodded. "I think I do. Did you always take this approach?"

"You mean me, personally? Or here at the store?"

He shrugged. "Both." He was more interested in the store, but he didn't want to alienate her. He was working on being more inclusive in his approach to... well... everyone. Three months ago, he would have written her off just because of her makeup, and here she was saying she was a Christian.

"Well, to be honest, I think originally the store was opened to help women look good on the outside because it boosts their confidence on the inside. But Miss Claire—she's my boss—she had some kind of epiphany a couple of months ago and decided to change a few things. She added these quotes around the store. She even changed the name of the store itself. It used to be Outside-In; now it's Inside-Out. Because now we're trying to help our clients find that balance between inner and outer beauty. You should hear her when she's talking to a client. Even if they don't buy anything, they leave here feeling more special and more attractive than they came in. She has some kind of gift, I think. She's done wonders helping me believe that God finds me valuable and beautiful."

Robert nodded his encouragement for her to keep speaking.

"And Miss Claire... well, she explained it to me, and it makes perfect sense. Besides, as Momma always says, 'Beauty is only skin-deep.'"

Robert was slow to respond. "I got you."

"Anyway, sir, I'm sure you didn't come in here to talk about our business philosophy." Mitzie grinned.

"No, I didn't, but I'm glad we had this little talk. I was actually looking for Claire." He smiled at her.

"Oh, she's not in at the moment. She went down to the food court."

"The food court?" He glanced at his watch. It wasn't quite eleven o'clock.

"Cupcake run." Mitzie winked at him. "We both adore cupcakes and those powdered mini donuts!"

"I see." He tucked the tidbit of information away in his mind for future reference.

"You're welcome to wait. I could give you a mini-facial, if you'd like. Men need to take care of their skin, too, you know. Or maybe you'd like to look at our skin care products. No offense, but you look like you could use a good exfoliant."

Robert could tell she was serious. "Maybe next time. I think I'll just head down to the food court and see if I can find Claire."

"No problem. Nice talking with you. Come back for that facial some time. And tell her not to hurry back!" She gave him a knowing smile.

Robert waved at Mitzie and headed out the door.

ෆ

The food court was crowded, but Robert zeroed in on As You Like It Pastry as soon as he stepped off the escalator. He immediately spotted Claire leaning against the counter as she chatted with a man who appeared to be the store manager. Like Mitzie, she was dressed in full black and in front of her was a paper sack that no doubt contained the pastries she had gone in search of.

The manager grinned at Claire, and Robert felt sick to his stomach. The man was looking at her like she was on the menu, and the more he spoke, the more Claire laughed. Robert shook his head. Had she ever shared a laugh with him? He sneered, disgusted with himself. What right did he have to be jealous over a woman he had rejected without even giving her a chance?

He stood close to the bottom of the escalator and contemplated whether or not he should go over there. He had been nervous when he'd gone into her store, and now he felt even worse. He might need a little more time to think about what he'd learned about her just by going to her business place.

Before he could make up his mind, the object of his thoughts materialized directly in front of him.

"Robert?" She was looking at him with a quizzical expression. She held a molded paper tray with two cups in one hand and the paper sack in the other. Now that she was close to him, he could see that her makeup was similar to Mitzie's. An experiment, her assistant had said.

"Claire, hi." He took his hands from his pockets and dried his damp palms on the sides of his pants. He didn't expect to be nervous!

"Are you okay? You look a little... lost."

He gave a tight smile. "I was... for a moment. Do you have a minute?" He pointed at an empty table close by.

"Actually, I have to get back to work." She lifted her hands and showed him what she was carrying.

"Claire... I... please. Just for a few minutes."

She hesitated a moment before shrugging.

They walked to the table, and she put the cups and paper bag down and allowed him to pull out her chair before she sat.

He moved to the spot across from her and took a deep breath as he sat. His mouth worked a little before he could find the right words to start the conversation he'd been anticipating for the past week or two. "Claire, I... it's good to see you. I was considering giving you a call, but... I wasn't sure you'd answer the phone."

She shrugged again. It was obvious that she was uncomfortable, and he couldn't say he blamed her. She reached for her cup and looked at him over the rim as she took a sip.

Robert couldn't help but think that even with her face under so much... stuff... she was still beautiful. Her eyes were so warm he could spend the rest of the day staring into them. Unsure what to say, he dived in. "Actually, I'm coming from your store. Your assistant—Mitzie, was it?— told me you might be down here." He wanted to ask how she was, but he hesitated. "It's been... a while," he said.

She gave a weak, condescending smile that didn't quite reach her black-rimmed eyes and remained silent. Her fingers tore little slits along the top of the paper bag. *What does she have to be nervous about?* Robert wondered. "How have you been?"

"Good. You?"

"I've been... thinking... about some things." He took another deep breath before continuing. "All right, let me just cut to the chase. The last time we saw each other, it didn't end well."

"To say the least," Claire agreed.

"And... well... you said some things that... some things that might be considered offensive."

Her eyes met his as she stopped in the middle of removing the cover from her paper cup, and Robert braced himself for another tongue-lashing from her. He was surprised when she sighed and placed the cover on a paper towel she had laid on the table before reaching into the sack and retrieving a couple packets of brown sugar. "You're right."

He almost did a double take. "I am?" He asked. In his wildest dreams, he'd never expected *that* to be her response.

"Yes." She tore both packets open at once and dumped the sugar into the cup and produced a stirrer. "You're right," she admitted as she slowly stirred the tea. "I said some really offensive things to you, and I'm sorry." She replaced the cover and looked up and into his eyes.

Robert wasn't sure how to respond. As often as he'd imagined this conversation, he'd never expected it to involve an apology from *her*. Before he could say anything, she continued.

"I mean… let's be clear here… some of it needed to be said, but I could have —*should have*—been more respectful in my approach."

Robert couldn't believe his ears. He still couldn't think of a response, which was just as well, because she wasn't finished.

"Ministers have to be prepared to meet people where they are, Robert. Even if you disapprove of their lifestyle, you've got to remember that God loves them. Pastors don't have the monopoly on grace. And the more grace you get, the more you should be giving, you know?"

She spoke slowly, as if choosing her words very carefully. "Some of the people we meet… they're going through stuff you and I can't even imagine. People like them… if you approach them the wrong way—even in the name of Christ, maybe even *especially* in the name of Christ—they'll shut right down on you and you won't ever get another chance. You might even be the one who turns them away from God and the church for good." Concern was etched across her face. "And I'm sure that's the last thing you want."

Robert reached into his shirt pocket for a stick of gum and popped it into his mouth, chewing thoughtfully. The message from her lips was familiar, and an image of Aunt Ruby came to mind. "Thank you."

A look of surprise crossed her face. "For?" she asked, before taking another sip.

"For putting it that way. I mean... I've been reflecting on what you said that day. I was pretty offended at first, but then I spoke to Aunt Ruby and she gave me some perspective."

"Yeah, she has a way of doing that, doesn't she?"

For the first time, Robert could tell that Claire's smile was genuine. He relaxed, but only a little. "Indeed. Anyway, I came here so *I* could apologize to *you.*"

She raised the cup to her dark purple lips, her eyes never leaving his.

"Claire, I'm really sorry."

She waited.

"I'm sorry for the things I've said to you. I'm sorry for making you the subject of that Bible study. I'm sorry for a lot of things. But mostly, I'm sorry for judging you just like you said I did. I was so busy pointing out what I thought was wrong with you when what I should have been doing was getting to know you for *you* and not for your appearance.

"You were absolutely right that day in the park. I had an image in my mind of what a good, Christian woman should look like, and because you didn't fit that mold, I dismissed you as some kind of sinner. I was ready to throw scripture—maybe even the whole Bible—at you, but I completely disregarded the verse that speaks of taking the beam out of my own eye before commenting on the speck of dust I thought I saw in yours." He folded the gum wrapper into halves and then into smaller and smaller triangles.

"My whole approach was wrong. *I* was wrong, and I regret it." He smiled ruefully, "You'll be glad to know I got a C for the Bible study." He smiled, and was rewarded with a chuckle from her.

"And with the stroke of the professor's pen, poetic justice has been served!" She burst out laughing, and before long, his own laughter mixed with hers.

This is nice, he thought. *I could get used to this.*

She recovered from her laughing fit and her face became serious again, causing Robert to sober up. "To be fair, your Bible study wasn't a complete failure."

"I suspect that's why I didn't get an outright F. Either that, or Dr. Crouch took pity on me."

"That's something you'd have to discuss with him; I can only tell you how it affected *me*." She swirled the cup and took another sip. "Those verses you shared... well, they spoke to me in a different way than they spoke to you. You were, to a certain extent, correct in your interpretation. I mean, a woman's beauty *should* radiate from her spirit. It *should* be more than skin-deep. Personally, I don't think that means she can't enhance her physical beauty—within reason—but for me, it means her inner beauty doesn't have to be the only thing she should be known for.

"I went and read the scriptures from your presentation, and after a lot of doubt and soul-searching, I compared them to the Proverbs thirty-one wife and mother we Christian women are always being encouraged to be. To me, it's clear that looks actually *are* important. It's one way of showing how God has blessed us. The Proverbs thirty-one woman was many things, but among them, it says she was clothed in fine linen. Do you see what I'm saying?" She regarded him over the rim of her cup again.

"I see what you're saying," he confirmed. "I guess it's about balance."

"Right. It's about balance and it's about keeping God in the center of *every* part of our life." She glanced at her watch and quickly got to her feet. "I'm sorry, I have to go. I have a client coming in at 11:30."

He stood and put his hands in his pockets as she dropped the sugar packets and stirrer into a nearby bin. Another deep breath. He wouldn't blame her if she thought he was asthmatic. "Claire, I was wondering... I'd like to continue this conversation... maybe over dinner?"

She hesitated for a long moment before she smiled. "I'll think about it. Call me," she said before heading towards the escalator.

Robert couldn't help but grin as he watched her hurry away. Those hips had a way of reminding him that, future minister or not, he was a man and not a statue.

◌

Robert hadn't felt this nervous on a first date in years. He'd gone on countless first dates, especially in the two or three years before going to seminary, but few had led to second dates. A third date was a true rarity for him. With his new perspective and self-awareness, he understood that his own unrealistic, unreasonable standards had clouded his vision over the years. That was what had led him to so many years of solitude. He liked to present himself as a man who was too busy for a social life, but he was beginning to see that he was hiding behind a mask he'd been wearing so long that he had started to think it was his real self.

He'd been attracted to several women who professed to be Christians, but something always held him back. The truth was that no woman had been good enough... modest enough... saved enough... holy enough... just *enough* for him to consider her worthy of the attentions of a man who was as sold out to the Lord as he figured he was. He looked at his reflection in the mirror as he tied his tie and shook his head. He'd been such a judgmental hypocrite—so caught up in himself that he had failed to see that he was falling short of his own calling to introduce Christ to those who didn't know Him.

Several times over the past weeks, he'd been tempted to fall into the trap of self-condemnation. He'd gotten into the habit of reminding himself over and over that with Christ, there was no condemnation for a heart that was truly repentant. Since God had forgiven him, he needed to forgive himself.

He finished with his tie and looked at his reflection in the full-length mirror on the back of the bathroom door. His gray paisley tie complemented his deep purple long-sleeved shirt and dark gray pants. He had cleaned and polished his black leather shoes until they gleamed. He stood there with his hands in his pockets and rocked back on his heels. He had to admit that the man looking back at him cleaned up nicely. Not only that, he was intelligent and accomplished—a college graduate, business owner and future pastor. Any woman would be proud to be by his side, not just tonight, but for the foreseeable future, as well.

"There I go again, Lord," Robert said aloud as he took note of his train of thought, "making myself out to be some kind of prize. As if I didn't know that I'm all kinds of messed up on the inside. Any and everything good in me—any and everything great that I ever accomplish—is a reflection of You. I've been so self-centered for so long that it's hard to break the habit, but I'm working on it, and I ask for Your grace to help me remember to be humble and lean on You. Not just tonight, but going forward."

He turned towards the dresser and chose a bottle of cologne. He sprayed only a light mist; he didn't want Claire walking around in a cologne cloud all night.

On his way through the door, he grabbed his wristwatch, cell phone and keys from the small entrance table. She only lived a couple of minutes away, so he didn't need to rush, but he didn't want to be late, either.

He started the car and shifted into reverse. He had made reservations at an intimate, but popular, seafood restaurant on Jacksonville Beach. He'd considered several options when trying to decide where to take Claire this evening. At first, he'd planned on heading to the historic town of St. Augustine less than an hour away. With its narrow streets and trolley cars, he knew many considered it perfect for a romantic date, but he didn't want to move too fast, nor did he want the setting to overshadow the opportunity they had to get to know each other. If things went well tonight, there would be lots more dates and more opportunities to take her on special outings.

He knew he'd wasted a lot of time judging Claire, and he hoped he hadn't done irreparable damage. The fact that she had agreed to go out with him—after everything—was a promising start. He prayed everything went well tonight. He wanted desperately to get to know her better, and things with them had gotten off to such a rocky start that this could very well be his last opportunity with her.

೮

Claire sat in front of her well-lit vanity and stared at her reflection in the mirror. She had her entire personal arsenal of makeup and tools in front of her, but thus far she had only applied primer and foundation. She wasn't sure what to do. She wanted to be attractive for her date with Robert, but she couldn't figure out what that meant to *him*. It was clear that he wasn't a fan of makeup, but where did that leave the makeup artist he'd invited to dinner?

When he'd called to make arrangements, he wouldn't tell her where they were going, only that she should "dress up." She wondered if he knew how vague that was for a woman. She'd chosen a deep purple, black, white, fuchsia dress with a geometric pattern. Its knee-length, halter-top style hugged her curves without being too revealing, and it always made her feel beautiful and feminine. She'd have liked to wear a dark, smoky eye to complement the look, but she wondered if that would be too much, considering this evening's company.

The clock on the wall told her Robert would be there in half an hour; she needed to get a move on. Should she go with the dramatic makeup or go with a subtler look? "Decisions, decisions," she muttered to herself.

She had seen the shock that had registered on his face at the mall when he had seen her makeup, but to his credit, he had remained a gentleman and hadn't asked any questions. Even after finding out that he'd had quite a long discussion with Mitzie earlier that morning, she wanted to believe that he really *had* seen the error of his ways and was interested in finding out who she really was beneath the blush and shadows. Still, she was anxious about tonight's date.

She hadn't forgotten that seismic shift she'd experienced at their first meeting, and her enduring curiosity was probably the only reason she had agreed to this date. Well… that and the fact that she was still more than a little bit infatuated with him!

Well, it was now or never. If he was going to date her, he needed to get to know the real Claire Foxwood. And the real Claire Foxwood had studied makeup artistry.

She leaned closer to the mirror and reached for her medium-sized round brush and dark gray eye shadow. Ten minutes later, she leaned back to look at the finished look. Her eyes were perfect. The dark purple, pale violet, dark grays and silver tones were the perfect combination to bring attention to her dark eyes. They were her favorite feature, and she liked to highlight them. She finished the look with a light cream bronzer and lips that were almost nude.

She stood and looked at herself in the antique cheval mirror in the corner of her bedroom. The overall effect was exactly what she had been going for. She looked feminine, sophisticated and confident. She only hoped the butterflies in her stomach would stay there.

As the doorbell chimed and Chaz started yapping, she slipped her feet into her black, high-heeled sandals and reached for her small black purse and a black cardigan. As she made her way to the front of the house, she whispered a prayer that the evening would go well. She couldn't help but think, *If this man knows what's good for him, his reaction* better *be an improvement on his last visit!*

Chapter Sixteen

Claire took a deep, calming breath before swinging the front door open and reaching for the handle of the screen door. All the effort she'd put into getting ready was rewarded by the undisguised masculine appreciation that crossed Robert's face when he looked at her. She stood there and waited patiently as his eyes skimmed her all the way from her flipped hairstyle down to the metallic purple nail polish on her toes.

She rested her hand on her hip and shifted her weight to one side before clearing her throat. His eyes flew up to meet hers. He had the decency to look a little bit guilty at having been caught ogling her curves. She raised her eyebrows, but inside she was doing a happy dance. She couldn't help but celebrate the fact that the man she found so attractive thought the same about her. He didn't need to say a word, but he opened his mouth anyway.

"Claire. You look…." He closed his mouth before trying again. "Wow! You look… amazing."

She smiled graciously. "Thank you. You're rather dashing, yourself. Do you have hidden cameras in my bedroom or something?"

The smile disappeared from his face and he took a step back, raising his arms defensively. "What?!" He was obviously confused.

She giggled. "We match," she explained, looking pointedly down at her dress and then over to his ensemble.

"Oh," he smiled, clearly relieved. "You got jokes."

She grinned. "I have my moments."

He was standing with both arms awkwardly behind his back and Claire wondered if he was hiding a bouquet of flowers. She burst out laughing when he produced a paper sack bearing the As You Like It logo. She accepted the gift and peeked inside.

"Red velvet cupcakes and powdered mini donuts?" She raised an eyebrow at him. It had been a week since they'd spoken at the mall, and she didn't remember sharing any of her pastry with him then. They had spoken on the phone a couple of times before she'd agreed to go out with him, but she was sure they hadn't spoken about donuts or cupcakes.

"Mitzie *may* have said something..." he admitted with a smile.

Claire wanted to ask, "And you remembered?" but instead, she smiled. "How sweet!"

"I have my moments." He threw her earlier words back at her and they both grinned.

She wasn't ready to invite him into her home just yet, so she said, "Just give me a moment to put these in the kitchen." She looked at Chaz, who was still sitting just inside the screen door. "Don't let him leave, Chaz. A man who brings dessert might just have a little potential."

Robert laughed as she disappeared inside. A moment later, she said goodbye to her dog and stepped onto the porch beside her date.

Robert extended his arm, which was bent at the elbow. "Shall we?"

She slipped her hand through the crook of his arm. "We shall."

ఆ

By the time they arrived at the two-story oceanfront restaurant, Robert didn't even remember how nervous he had been earlier. The conversation with Claire had flowed smoothly in the car, and he was surprised at how comfortable he felt with her. While he was driving, her question about how he had met Aunt Ruby and Aunt Emmy had led to an edited version of his first direct encounter with them at the church. He'd never shared the story of the moment he had received his calling with anyone, and he certainly wouldn't be telling anyone on a first date. He did, however, tell her how surprised he had been when he found out that Aunt Emmy was the mother of his friend Daniel, whom he had known since high school. The two had lost touch after graduation, so Robert was pleasantly surprised when he'd seen a photo of Daniel on the wall the first time he had visited Aunt Ruby's home.

In the last few minutes of their journey to the restaurant, he had also told her about his childhood in Jacksonville and the loss of both his parents in his early twenties. He didn't have much family left—only a few cousins scattered all over the world.

He felt as if he could talk with her for hours and never run out of things to say. He could get used to this.

ભ

The restaurant had only been open for a few months, and neither Robert nor Claire had eaten there before. Robert had reserved a table on the deck upstairs, and Claire was glad she had her cardigan on what turned out to be a cool, windy evening. Her hair kept blowing into her face, but she didn't mind. The panoramic scene in front of her was worth it.

Night had already fallen on the city of Jacksonville, and as they sat, both Claire and Robert spent a few moments enjoying the awesome view. The lights all along Jacksonville Beach looked like diamonds on a black velvet backdrop. Being so close to the ocean made Claire feel small, but instead of questioning her significance in such a large universe, she felt humbled that the Lord who had created everything still took time to commune with her. She sent up a silent prayer, admitting that she was awed by God's love for her.

Robert was just as silent as she was, and Claire couldn't help but wonder what he was thinking. Just when she was about to ask, he murmured, "I don't understand how people can see all this and choose not to believe in God."

Claire nodded in agreement. They made eye contact, and Robert held her stare until the server came to take their drink order. Claire felt as if something significant had happened as they looked at each other across the table, but she wasn't quite sure what. She shivered as goose bumps covered her arms despite the cardigan.

β

Across the table, Robert found himself fighting the urge to reach over and push some of Claire's hair behind her ear. He wondered if she even knew how often she was brushing it out of her eyes. She was beyond beautiful. Her cheekbones were high, and she had done something to make them glow. Her eyes truly were the windows to her soul. Looking at her across the table, Robert felt as if he was the most blessed man in the room.

He couldn't quite explain it. She wasn't looking at him with desire or anything like that; instead, he wanted to believe that when she looked at him like that, she could see beyond all his faults and flaws and look directly at his heart. He'd never experienced anything quite like it.

The moment was shattered when the server appeared at their table, and he found himself almost shooing the young lady away. He tried to focus as she listed the evening's specials, but he found both his eyes and his attention wandering back to the woman who sat only a few feet away from him.

All the menu items were tempting, and they both had a hard time choosing. Claire eventually settled on seafood linguine in a light white wine sauce while Robert had grilled salmon with lemon and capers in a savory butter sauce. He was hard-pressed to remember the last time he'd had such a tasty meal.

Like the clam chowder they both had to start, their entrees were delicious, and Robert had to stop himself from reaching over and tasting some of her pasta. An hour flew by as they enjoyed the meal and their conversation, and he kept having to remind himself that she wasn't his girlfriend. This was only their first date. *Robert,* he silently cautioned himself, *don't get ahead of yourself.*

He listened intently and asked lots of questions about her childhood in Chicago and her decision to move so far away from most of her family. He was surprised that such a smart woman hadn't gone straight to college after school, but as she talked, he began to understand Claire's motivations for many of the decisions she had taken. He already knew that she was intelligent, but now he was being allowed some insight into her way of thinking, as well as how she had lived her life up to this point. She was amazing.

They were so full that they both declined dessert, and when Robert had attended to the check, their server advised them that many of their guests enjoyed a walk on the restaurant's private pier after their meal.

☙

Claire sat on a bench at the entrance to the pier to remove her sandals. She didn't want to risk hurting herself with her four-inch stilettoes on the pier's wooden slats.

Her movements were awkward as she tried to maintain her ladylike posture while bending over to attend to the task; even so, her mouth fell open when Robert asked, "May I?" before stooping low to unstrap the buckles at her ankles.

The movement was innocent but quite intimate, and Claire felt her entire body becoming warm as the gentle breeze caused Robert's tie to move against the tops of her feet.

When he got to his feet, she remained seated instead of standing. "Robert, I...." She wasn't quite sure how to approach the topic.

"Yes?" His expression was hard to read as he looked at her sitting in the shadows.

Why did he have to look so handsome? He was distracting her from what she wanted to say. It was an awkward topic to raise on a first date, but more than ever, she needed for him to know who she was and what was important to her.

"I... I'm having a really good time with you." She could see his white teeth as he smiled. "But there's something I need to... say."

"Okay." He dropped her sandals on the far end of the bench, sat beside her and turned to face her, his arm along the back of the bench and his face so close to hers that she could feel his breath on her cheek.

She looked towards the sea, where telltale lights betrayed the location of several yachts in the distance. "I know you're a Christian, but... well... I've dated men before who say they're saved and... they still have certain... expectations." She stopped again, unsure of how to proceed. "Well, the thing is, Robert, I'm celibate."

"Celibate?" His tone was incredulous, and Claire's spirit sank a little. Was that disappointment in his voice?

She was afraid to look at him, so she continued to stare at the Atlantic Ocean. "Yes. I don't intend to have sex with anyone until my wedding night."

Robert's response was to chuckle, which infuriated Claire. How dare he make fun of her decision? And just when she thought they were off to a good start, too!

She started to get to her feet, but Robert loosely held on to her wrist. She sat and forced herself to relax her jaw from its clenched position.

"Claire, relax. It's okay." His tone was light. "I'm celibate, too."

"You... you are?" She turned to face him, but he was still too close for comfort, so she turned back towards the view, chose a yacht with bright lights and stared at it.

"Of course, I am. I laughed because I was surprised you felt the need to tell me that." He held her hand between his. "I mean, I would think it was kind of obvious, but I understand. Not everybody who calls themselves a Christian believes in celibacy these days.

"As for me, I'm sold out to the Lord, Claire. I'm not going to pretend that I'm a virgin, but I decided years ago that I would not be going down that road again until and unless I'm married. I don't want to be that pastor who looks good in the pulpit but has to worry about the skeletons in his closet jumping out some day. So no worries there, okay?"

"Okay." Claire breathed an audible sigh of relief and relaxed against the back of the bench. His arm was warm.

"Now, what was that you were saying about having a good time with me?" He leaned even closer to her and she wondered if he was thinking about kissing her. She wasn't ready for that. Her emotions were already swirling around too much.

Claire felt her cheeks warm and she was glad he couldn't see her blushing. "Weren't we going for a walk on the pier?"

"Coward." Robert whispered in her ear before getting to his feet, his warm breath causing her entire body to quiver. Without relinquishing her hand, he scooped her sandals up and they headed for the pier.

Claire found herself becoming more and more at ease as the evening progressed. More than once, she thought to herself, *I could get used to this.*

ଓଃ

Two weeks later, Claire had to admit to herself that she was hooked. Having just got home from church, she found herself relaxing in her beloved recliner reminiscing about their two dates and completely ignoring the book in her lap.

They had spent over an hour leaning against the railing of the pier that first night. She was sure they hadn't left any stones unturned, but after the chaste hug they shared that night, they'd still managed to chat on the phone for another hour before reluctantly hanging up. They both had church the next morning.

The following Saturday, one of their favorite gospel groups was having a concert in Jacksonville, and they were there in row sixteen. It was an anointed worship experience, and at one point Claire became so overwhelmed that tears streamed down her face. Even with waterproof mascara, she knew she must have looked a sight. She was grateful that the lights were directed toward the stage. She looked over at Robert, concerned he might be staring at her like she was some kind of two-headed beast, but he only handed her his handkerchief and stood there with his strong arm around her shoulders and his attention on the stage. It was clear that he was having his own 'God moment,' as well.

Afterwards, he walked her to her door and grinned when she got the handkerchief from her bag. She noticed how soiled it had become, and cringed inwardly at the streaks of foundation, blush and eye makeup. It was too late to hide it in her bag, so she shrugged her shoulders and tried to avoid eye contact.

"Wow. That's a *lot* of… stuff."

"Yeah," she replied, hoping the awkward moment would pass quickly.

"You know, Claire, it would be hypocritical of me to stand here and pretend that I understand why you feel you need all of the… stuff; I don't. But none of that matters to me at this point. No amount of … *stuff* could make you more beautiful to me, and not wearing it wouldn't make you any less attractive. You're beautiful from the inside out. That's why I'm here."

Claire was speechless, but just when she was sure he was going to take her in his arms, he winked at her, said good night and slipped away. She almost stomped her foot in disappointment. How long was he going to make her wait before he kissed her? That had been a week ago yesterday, and although they spoke often, they hadn't seen each other since then.

She was still reflecting when her landline rang. She reached over and picked it up. "Hello?"

"Hi." His voice made her smile, but the fact that he hadn't felt the need to identify himself made her feel as if they had crossed over an invisible threshold in their relationship.

"Hi. Were you trying to call my cell phone?" She looked over at the sofa, where she had dropped her oversized 'church bag' half an hour earlier.

"Well… no, actually. I… I didn't think you were home yet. I was actually planning to leave a message on your answering machine."

Claire used the lever at the side of the recliner to drop the foot rest as she sat upright. This was weird. What could he possibly have to say that warranted a discussion with a machine? "Would you like me to hang up so you can call my machine?"

He chuckled. "No, that's okay. It's just that... well, I know it's last-minute and I kind of wanted to leave the message so you wouldn't feel pressured into answering right away.

"Would you like me to hang up?" she asked again. She hoped he was going somewhere with this, because right now she was more annoyed than intrigued.

"I... okay, here goes: do you remember come-as-you-are parties? I'm in the middle of cooking dinner and I was wondering if maybe you'd like to come over."

Claire thought of the beef stew simmering in her slow cooker. She had started it before church, and it would probably be ready in another thirty minutes. The aroma was permeating the whole house, causing her stomach to growl. There was jasmine vegetable rice in the rice cooker and a pasta salad chilling in the fridge.

"And the answering machine?"

"Well, I was going to say, 'Hey, Claire, I was wondering if you'd like to come over for a come-as-you-are dinner tonight. Just the two of us. If you're interested, give me a call, but don't feel bad if you can't make it. I know it's really last-minute. If I don't hear from you, I'll assume you had other plans.'"

Claire couldn't decide whether to be excited or afraid. She wanted to spend more time with him, but she wasn't sure about going to his apartment so soon. Although they had both chosen a celibate lifestyle, she didn't think it was smart to be cooped up in a small, private space with someone she found so attractive. She imagined them bumping into each other all the time, and that couldn't be good, right?

"I have a table set up on my back deck. The space is pretty small but it overlooks the swimming pool. Sunday afternoon like this, there'll probably be a couple of families out there."

She smiled. Had he been reading her mind? Or was it possible that he had the same concerns she did?

"Well, I *was* cooking, but…" her words trailed off.

"Please, Claire?" he pleaded. "I just want to spend a little more time with you."

She took a deep breath. It wasn't fair what this man could do to her with his voice… even when he wasn't sitting right by her ear. She felt a shiver run through her body as she remembered that night by the pier.

"Well… all right. I guess my dinner will keep till tomorrow." If they were outside, she should be okay.

Robert sounded so excited. "Should I come pick you up?"

"No, I'll walk. You should stay right where you are, slaving over that hot stove. You better have quite a spread ready for me."

She returned the phone to the cradle and looked down at her clothes. She had slipped on a tank top and a pair of shorts after church. "Come-as-you-are party?" she muttered. "He must be delusional!"

She was the kind of woman who liked having a lot of notice so she could figure out exactly what she was wearing, but she wasn't in the mood to go all out today.

She leaned over to give Chaz a quick tummy rub then got to her feet. She peeped through the glass cover of the slow cooker. She could see the gravy bubbling around chunks of beef and root vegetables. Robert better be *some* cook, for her to leave this at home.

She chose a pair of floral capri pants and an understated sleeveless white top. She had removed her makeup after church, so she quickly applied a tinted moisturizer, mascara and a shimmery light pink lipstick.

Just before heading out the door, she slipped her feet into casual slides and turned off the slow cooker.

⚃

Robert lifted the lid of the pot and checked the jambalaya. Perfect. He turned off the burner and turned his attention to the oven. He reached in with his left hand and got his hand halfway around the handle of the cast iron skillet before jumping back.

"Darn it!" he yelled. He had forgotten to use a pot holder. "Stupid! Stupid! Stupid!" he berated himself as he used his right hand to turn on the cold water. He stuck his left hand under the flow and racked his brain trying to remember how to treat this kind of burn.

Naturally, the doorbell rang just as he was standing there. He would have liked for everything to be perfect when Claire arrived, but serve him right for thinking of this at the last minute.

"It's open! Come on in!" he shouted in the direction of the front door.

The door creaked opened, and he turned from his position of the sink to greet Claire. She looked somewhat angelic, standing in the doorway with the afternoon sunlight behind her.

"Hey."

"What happened?" Her eyes zoned in on his hand under the water, and she closed the door before moving swiftly through the open concept room into the kitchen area.

"Burn. Could you do me a favor and turn off the oven?" He pointed towards the correct knob on the front of the stove. It smelled like his cornbread was starting to burn.

She did as he asked. "Pot holder?"

He pointed to the hook under the cabinet and watched as she deftly *and safely* removed the skillet from the oven. After placing it on the stove, she turned her attention to his hand.

Grabbing a towel from the counter, she came to stand beside him and placed her hand on his arm. He turned off the water and moved his hand so she could have a look. His palm was red, but he hadn't managed to close his hand around the skillet's handle, so the skin was intact.

"Hey. Why don't you sit down and let me take care of this?" Claire suggested as she led him to the rectangular table between the living room and kitchen.

"It doesn't hurt… too much." Robert hated appearing vulnerable in front of her.

"I didn't say it did. Where are your zip-top bags?"

He showed her which drawer to look in and she filled one with ice from the freezer before wrapping it in a towel. Sitting in the chair next to his, she held his hand in hers and applied the ice pack to his palm.

"How's that?" she asked, her eyes full of concern.

"Perfect." Robert wasn't looking at his palm; he was looking straight into her eyes.

She blushed and was about to turn away when he placed his good hand under her chin and prevented her from moving her face.

"Claire, I…" he worked his throat as he tried to find words. He had spent more time speechless in her presence than around all his teenage crushes combined.

The discomfort forgotten, he leaned towards her, stopping a few inches from her face to give her the opportunity to stop him if she wanted to.

Apparently, she didn't want to. Instead, her movements mirrored his until their lips met in a sweet embrace.

Robert smiled against her mouth. Her lips were soft and tasted like watermelon-flavored chewing gum, not strawberries as he had anticipated. He angled his head, his mouth slanting against hers as she opened to give him access. His left hand curved against her neck as he moved to deepen the kiss even more, and he got a painful reminder of his accident.

He snapped his head back. "Ouch!"

"Ouch?" Claire wrinkled her brow and he raised his palm so she could see it. He retrieved the abandoned ice pack and closed his hand around it. So she had forgotten the burn, too. He took that as a good sign.

"Oh, Robert! I'm sorry, I—"

He silenced her with another sweet, lengthy kiss before his hormones woke up and reminded him of the promise he had made to God years ago. He reluctantly pulled away from her and got to his feet, needing to put some distance between them.

She smiled shyly in his direction before clearing her throat. "How's your hand?"

"I'll survive." He smiled in her direction as he moved back towards the stove. "There went my plan to impress you with my amazing culinary skills."

"You don't need to impress me, but if it makes you happy, your cornbread looks fantastic even with the brown edges. And what is that wonderful smell?"

He grinned. Claire Foxwood looked good in his apartment. She looked good in his life. As he used his right hand to reach for a couple of bowls, he thought, *I could* really *get used to this.*

CHAPTER SEVENTEEN

Eighteen months later

Robert had no idea what Claire had been praying for, but for his part, it was clear that the Lord had sent him the woman who would stand beside him for the rest of his life. Claire tended to be outspoken in disagreements with him, but he had come to appreciate that she was just as vocal in her support of him and his efforts. Things between them were imperfectly perfect, and the love between them was obvious. He'd always thought it was cliché before, but now he understood what other men meant when they said their woman made them want to be a better man. He definitely felt that way about Claire. Even more than that, he felt as if God was using her to help him fulfill his purpose, and that was the best feeling in the world. He hoped he would never lose sight of that.

For the last year or so, he had been serving as youth pastor for his church. One Sunday after service, the pastor asked to speak with him.

As Robert sat waiting in the upholstered chair in the pastor's office, he wondered what Dr. Johnstone wanted to see him about. Everyone knew that Doc never had meetings on a Sunday, so Robert imagined this must be pretty urgent. He retrieved a handkerchief from his pocket and wiped his sweaty palms. Hearing the minister entering the room, he stood and stuffed the square of cloth into his pocket.

"Sit down, sit down, Robert," Dr. Johnstone grinned as he circled the desk and took his own seat.

"How are you, Doc?" Robert asked. He had always liked his pastor. Although he had been preaching for over twenty years and had several degrees in ministry, Dr. Jefferson Johnstone was an affable man with a heart for the people.

"Good! Good!" Doc's voice boomed. "You?"

"I'm doing very well, thanks."

"So I've noticed, so I've noticed." He nodded his head. "You must be wondering why I called you in here today, but I've been putting something off, and the Lord has impressed upon me that it must be done today." He steepled his fingers on the desk in front of him and looked at Robert with a serious expression on his face. "You know, son, as much as possible, you should do what God tells you to do, when He tells you to do it. Don't delay, because then He might have to strike you, and if God strikes you, my son, you are well struck!"

The pastor dissolved into laughter, but Robert remained stoic. Was there something God had told him to do that he hadn't done? He searched his recollection while the pastor laughed, but came up with nothing.

"Don't worry, son. That message was for me, not you." The pastor's face became serious again. "For the past few weeks—months, really—the Lord has been laying it on my heart to share something with you. I kept putting it off and putting it off, but this morning, like I said, He told me, 'Jefferson, today is the day. Don't you let that boy go home without talking with him!'"

He opened a drawer and took out a folder with a transparent front cover. It rested in both his hands for a few seconds before the minister sighed and handed it over to Robert. Robert took it and noticed that the photo on the front featured an architectural mock-up of what looked like a town. He looked at his pastor, eyebrows raised.

"A friend of mine from out of town is planning to develop some land not too far from here. Ryland and I go way back, and he's been developing real estate all over the lower East Coast. But this here will be his pride and joy."

Robert looked up from the folder, all sorts of questions racing through his mind.

"He and his wife are God-fearing people. When I say they love the Lord, I mean they *love* the Lord. They've always been shrewd in business, while being fair in their dealings with everybody. As a result, they are stinkin', filthy rich, as some folks would say."

Robert had no idea where he was going with this information.

"He called me up a couple of months ago and told me about this project he's working on. Said he wanted to build a community for families. He made me a proposal, and I will tell you I wanted to jump on it. I wanted it to be mine. But it wasn't. At first God wouldn't give me any peace about it. Then every time I thought about it… every time I prayed about it, your face would come up in my spirit." He sighed loudly. "But I still wanted the blessing and the promise to be mine. So I kept delaying, hoping the Lord would change His mind, I guess. But no can do."

Robert was confused. Just as he was about to seek clarity, Doc continued.

"In your hands, you are holding a proposal for a neighborhood called Alistair Bay, named for Ryland Bay's parents. It's located outside of St. Augustine. Ground has been broken and construction is already underway. If you'll have a look at the plans, you'll see that the town itself surrounds a huge park, and then houses will be built on the periphery of the commercial area. Ryland figures within about five years, there will be several hundred families living there. Those families will need education, so they're building three schools. They'll need medical care, so they're building a medical center. They'll also need Jesus... and that's where you come in." In response to Robert's unspoken question, Doc continued, "They're building three churches, and I'm recommending that they offer you a position in one of them. As pastor."

"Come again?" Robert wasn't sure he was hearing right.

"I've seen your development over the last year. I've seen you serve, even when you thought nobody was watching you. You do things as onto the Lord, and I think you're ready to shepherd your own flock, son. The Lord has been telling me to turn this opportunity over to you."

"I don't know what to say."

"Well, I do. Say you'll pray about it. Then say you'll say yes."

"But how...?"

"Ryland and his wife have a foundation, and there will be a sizable grant for each church.... Just to help cover the initial costs and cover some expenses until things level off and the church is able to meet its own expenses."

"But how...?" Robert wasn't even sure what he wanted to ask.

"It's all God, Robert. I've been here for ten years, and I could do with a change of scenery... a fresh start. I would have jumped at the opportunity, but God made it clear that this is not *my* open door; it's yours."

For the first time, Robert looked closely at the portfolio in his hand. Turning the pages, he saw Victorian-style houses, quaint shops, and the park Doc said would be the central feature of the neighborhood. He saw artists' impressions of churches with people milling around in front of them, but when he saw the brick one with white trim and the steeple on top, it was as if it was speaking to him. His brain felt as if it had been flooded with information. He snapped the folder shut and looked up into the eyes of his pastor, unsure of what to say.

"Now, I want to be clear, Robert: I will give you as much help as I can, but essentially, you will be planting your own church. Ryland wants two major denominations — the Catholics and another major protestant group like the Methodists, Baptists or Episcopalians, but he also wants a third church that is fresh and new and non-denominational. I told him you're the man for the job."

"Wha — ?"

"The option is yours to take it or leave it, but it's as good as yours. He trusts my judgment and he trusts God's divine leading."

"But I'm not — " Robert still wasn't sure what to say, but he knew he felt inadequate.

Doc got to his feet and came around the desk to place his beefy hand on Robert's shoulder. "Son, I know this is coming at you from left field, but I want you to remember that God's favor can do in a moment what your labor couldn't do in a lifetime. You're ready. Now, go home, fast and pray, and seek the Lord's wisdom in this, and then in a few days, let me know what you want to do. Say the word, and I will drive you out to the site to meet Ryland and start the ball rolling. It's going to take another year or two for everything to be ready, and I really do think that by the time Alistair Bay is ready for you, you'll be just as ready for Alistair Bay."

Robert stood and shook the pastor's hand. "Thank you, Doc. I... I guess I'll call you in a few days."

"Wonderful. Now, before you go... how's that young lady of yours?"

Robert felt the smile breaking across his face. "She's fine, thank you, Doc. Probably wondering why I'm late for Sunday dinner."

"Mighty fine woman you've got there."

"I know it, sir."

"You said she's earning a degree in something?"

"Yes, sir. She's just starting her bachelor's and she hopes to go straight into a master's degree in social work. She's a makeup artist by profession, but she's enjoying her work at the community center and the nursing home. There's talk of her working at the center full-time."

"I see."

As the younger man placed his hand on the door handle to take his leave, the pastor's next words knocked the wind out of him. "Oh, and by the way, those families will need a community center. And that community center will need an administrator."

As Robert turned to look at him, Doc grinned and waved.

೦೩

Claire was concerned. This had been her longest relationship to date, and she had no doubt Robert was the man for her. She was sure their relationship was destined for marriage, and until recently, Robert had seemed to agree. For the last few weeks, however, every time she brought up the subject of marriage, he seemed to be putting her off. When he called her up one Saturday night and told her they needed to talk after church, she got that sinking feeling in her stomach that something was terribly wrong. Was there a problem? A major one?

He'd been somewhat distant lately. He had turned down three recent invitations to come for dinner, telling her he was in a period of prayer and fasting concerning his future. He kept telling her that he couldn't see her as much as he used to because he needed some time alone with God. He never called her unless she called him first, and his responses to her text messages were brief and dismissive.

She was more than concerned; she was a little worried.

This was the man whose destiny was all tied up in hers. This was the man she could see herself sharing her life with. She didn't relish the idea of being the submissive wife, but if ever there was a man who could love his wife like Christ loved the church, she was convinced that Robert Marsden was the one.

She couldn't deny that this was the man who seemed to have taken up permanent residence on her very last nerve, but she didn't want it any other way. She didn't want to be without him. "He *better* not be breaking up with—" she said out loud as she slipped off the African print wrap dress she'd worn to church. "No! I'm not even going to think that. There's got to be something else going on with him."

She slipped on a casual halter dress in fuchsia. She liked her shoulders, and preferred to wear halter tops when they were practical. Strappy gold sandals took the place of her four-inch heels, and she had added a headband to her braided style.

Chaz ran towards the door before the doorbell rang, and she took a deep breath before opening it. Robert looked pensive as he greeted her and brushed a chaste kiss across her cheek. They had both agreed that sex would not be a part of their relationship at this point, but they enjoyed their fair share of passionate kisses. This was not one of them. She swallowed with difficulty and stepped backward to allow Robert access into her home.

"Actually, I wondered if you would like to go for a drive with me. There's something I want to show you."

At least he hadn't said that there was something he wanted to discuss with her.

"Am I dressed okay?" She looked doubtfully at his suit.

"You're fine. I came straight here from church. We ran a little late today."

His church was almost always 'running late.' It was one of the reasons she hadn't wanted to transfer there. Her service started at nine and ended before twelve, while Robert's church started at eight and usually went past two o'clock. By the time she got out of his service, all she wanted to do was nap.

They drove in uncomfortable silence. After five minutes, he slipped in one of their favorite jazz CDs and she closed her eyes. She was surprised when she heard him calling her name what felt like a few minutes later, only to take note that she had dozed off for more than half an hour. Completely disoriented, she looked around. She recognized nothing... not that there was anything to recognize, really.

He had parked on a street—if you could call it that, since it wasn't actually paved—that was surrounded with... what, exactly? Claire was confused. On one side of the road, heavy duty landscaping equipment was parked among huge mounds of dirt. All around her were buildings in various stages of construction.

For a moment, she wondered if they had missed the Rapture. Despite the equipment, everything was silent, as if all the construction workers had been snatched up in the middle of their tasks. The place was deserted, except for the two of them.

"Where are we?" she asked after he got out and came around to open her door.

"Alistair Bay, Florida."

"Alistair Bay? I've never heard of it."

Robert smiled and took hold of her elbow before piloting her across the street. They both stood in front of a building that looked like all the others except for the huge parking lot on one side of it.

"Robert, what's—?"

"I'll explain in a few minutes. I promise, everything will be clear soon enough. You're standing next to the foundation of the future Alistair Bay New Covenant Community Fellowship."

"Ooookaaay." Her response signaled her lack of clarity on the matter.

"Over there—," he waved his arm at a portion of land on the far side of the dirt mounds that was still bare, "— is where they're going to put the Margaret Alistair Bay Community Center."

"Ooookaaay." She was dying with curiosity, but she had come to understand that Robert Marsden did and said things in his own time, so it made no use trying to hurry him along.

"I want you to take a good look at everything you see here, because in a few months, it will all look quite different."

"Ooookaaay."

He guided her back to the car and they took a quick drive away from the hub of construction and towards a field of what appeared to be corn that was divided by several tracks that crisscrossed their way through it.

"Robert, what—"

He smiled again, but said nothing. Before too long, he stopped the car in the middle of the track he had been driving in and stepped out. Claire noticed that he took a deep breath before opening her door, something that always made her feel cherished and special. She stepped out and cringed as her sandaled foot made contact with the track. She hated the feeling of dust between her toes.

As they both stood in the middle of the trail, Robert indicated a part of the field that formed a corner where two tracks intersected.

"Sweetheart, I know it doesn't look like much now, but within the next year, if the Lord tarries, this entire field will be replaced by single family homes and duplexes. And right here, on this spot, will stand a four-bedroom Victorian-style home with a two-car garage hidden in the back and a porch swing to one side. Can you see it?"

Claire could only see what appeared to be acres and acres of corn, but she didn't think it was prudent to say so, so she shrugged.

"Claire Foxwood, two days ago, I went all in on a dream. I sold just under half the shares in my bookstore last month, and I used the cash I got, added some of my savings, and made a down payment on a house lot. *This* house lot."

Claire took a sharp breath. He did *what*?

He continued, "Now, I know I should have discussed this with you before I did it, but I felt the sure leading of the Holy Spirit in this matter. He told me exactly what I needed to do.

"As the Lord would have it, I've already signed the paperwork to start our own church right here in Alistair Bay. Like I said, it's going to be called the New Covenant Community Fellowship. I am to be its pastor. And..." he stuttered, "I want you to be its first lady."

"Say what?" Claire was beyond confused. Alistair Bay... house lots... church... pastor... first lady? What was Robert going on about?

Claire looked at the field of corn in front of her again and then back at Robert.

As she watched with her mouth open, he dropped to one knee in the middle of the dirt track and produced a tiny velvet box.

"Claire Foxwood, I love you. I have loved you since the beginning of time. I loved you on the day you were born. I loved you on the day you took your first step and on the day you had your heart broken by the first boy you ever liked. I loved you when you graduated from high school, and I loved you when you walked into that office and registered for your undergraduate degree.

"I loved you the moment I saw you in that ridiculous Big Bird get-up, even though I didn't know it then. I loved you when I was too busy judging you. I loved you when you forgave me even when I didn't know I was wrong. I love you when you upset me and when I upset you. I already love the wife you will be to me, and the mother you will be to the children I hope we'll be blessed with. I love you.

"I want to spend the rest of my life loving you and making you blush, and maybe even driving you crazy. Even if you say no to me today, I will still continue to love you because I believe beyond a shadow of a doubt that loving you was one of the things I was born to do.

"When I first met you, I was a different person. I thought that you were my last resort. Little did I know then how right I was." Before Claire could react, he rushed on, "You're my last resort, my first resort, and every one in the middle. I'm convinced that you're the woman God had in mind when he created me. I'm the man He had in mind when He created you.

"Claire Foxwood, will you do me the honor of marrying me? Will you plant a church with me? Will you build not only a house but a future with me? Will you stand beside me and in front of me and behind me all our lives? Will you love me past my faults? Will you lead me to a greater knowledge of God as I do the same for you? Will you allow God to love you through me?"

Claire was overwhelmed. Was Robert actually proposing all these things to her? Was he actually proposing marriage?

She took a deep breath. "Nothing would make me happier than marrying you, planting a church with you, building a house with you... and... everything else you said. Nothing would bring me more joy than being your partner in life and allowing God to love you through me. I love you, Robert Marsden. I *love* you."

He chuckled. "I guess that was a yes?"

"Yes!" She shouted. "Yes! Yes! *Yes!*"

As he rose and crushed her to him in a deep kiss that promised her a lifetime of love, she was flooded with a peace she couldn't explain. She couldn't—wouldn't—have admitted it then, but this was exactly what she had wanted from that very first day she had opened her door and seen him standing there.

When the two of them came up for air, she said. "Now, what were you saying about four bedrooms? We'll need at least five—one for each of the three kids and one for when my parents come to visit."

Robert laughed and hugged her to him. "I might consider that, but it depends."

"On?"

"On how attached you are to that ridiculous Big Bird robe!"

The End

DEAR READER...

You can't imagine how humbled I am that you've taken the time to read *His Last Resort*. I really hope you enjoyed it, and that it has blessed you in some way. It never ceases to amaze me that God would use my imagination as a channel to share His Word with others, and I don't take it for granted.

His Last Resort is the first book in the *His Last Hope Series*, and is the prequel to my debut novel, *His Last Hope*. If you haven't already done so, I encourage you to pick up a copy of *His Last Hope*, which is now Book Two in the series.

In *His Last Hope*, a pregnant amnesiac is taken in by Aunt Ruby, much to the chagrin of her widowed nephew Daniel. Having been taken advantage of before, Daniel doesn't trust easily, and fears that the mystery woman wants to exploit his aunt's kindness.

As if that isn't enough, the trio and their closest friends must deal with an unexpected tragedy that could destroy them emotionally. Will it bring them closer to each other and to God? Or will Daniel find another reason to distance himself from his Maker? What will happen when Daniel finds himself falling for "Hope"? Will any of them ever find out who she really is and whose child she's carrying? What will Daniel do when someone turns up to claim her?

Find out what happens in *His Last Hope*, the book the Christian Small Publishers Association named their 2016 Romance Book of the Year.

And one last thing: would you be so kind as to leave a review of *His Last Resort* on Amazon or Goodreads? Reviews help increase visibility so readers can find the perfect books for them.

I appreciate you more than you know!

Blessings,
M. A. Malcolm

HIS LAST RESORT GROUP DISCUSSION GUIDE

1. Claire struggled with self-esteem issues as a young lady; how might Robert have adjusted his study of the same scriptures (1 Peter 3:1-12 and 1 Timothy 2:8-10) to encourage women like her instead of discourage them?

2. Can you think of any scriptures that would encourage a Christian who has been struggling with low self-esteem for a long time?

3. Aunt Ruby seems to be a real fountain of godly wisdom; what do you think it takes to be able to speak about scripture with such authority? Do you know anyone like Aunt Ruby?

4. Throughout the first few chapters, Robert displays a distinct 'holier-than'thou' attitude. How could that kind of approach affect his future ministry?

5. Do you think pastors who consider congregants' feelings before delivering a sermon are 'watering down' the importance of a having contrite, repentant spirit? Is it ever appropriate for a pastor to preach a sermon that scares people into repentance? Illustrate your response with examples and scenarios.

6. Aunt Ruby encourages Claire to read the Bible for herself rather than depend wholly on others to interpret its message for her. To what extent do you believe the average Christian can correctly interpret scriptures for themselves?

7. Can you think of any popular sayings that are attributed to the Bible, but aren't actually found within its pages?

8. What are your views on women wearing makeup? Have your views changed after reading *His Last Resort*? Why or why not?

9. The author used opposing views on appearance as a vehicle to focus on a much wider message; what do you think that message was? Can you think of other vehicles the author could have used?

10. Can you think of real-life examples where people who might not be embraced by the church have used their unexpected gifts to bring glory to God?

11. What other scripture(s) could the author have used as a central theme for *His Last Resort*?

ACKNOWLEDGEMENTS

I stand in awe of my 'Holy Ghostwriter,' who has chosen me 'for such a time like this' to be one of the channels of His messages. It never ceases to amaze me that the Lord would use a broken vessel like me to be a conduit for His glory.

I would also like to thank the following people for their support and input:

- Radford and Kareem—for not complaining during those times when my writing got in the way of my 'wife-ing' and mothering.
- My parents, Churnley and Beryl Gray, for being the best sales team a writer ever had! I appreciate your unwavering love, support and commitment in every area of my life.
- My bonus Mommy, Renita Patrick—for the way you love me.
- My siblings, bonus siblings and their families—for your encouragement and interest. Your endorsement means the world to me.
- Too many cousins and friends to list—for not letting me quit!
- Robin, Oliver and Romar of Faith in Christ Ministries, Inc.—for your friendship and spiritual leading for more than a decade. Loveremains ;)
- My beta readers: Tracia, Nichole, Chrissy, Marsha C., Lauren, Rochelle, Robin and Natasha—for your willingness and honesty.
- Soraya and Cecile—your simple act of kindness has boosted my spirits more than you could ever know! I still have rice and peas in my freezer. ;)
- Every reader who took the time to read my work, recommend it to others and demand more—*His Last Resort* is all your fault!
- My mailing list subscribers and social media followers—for the encouragement, the feedback and the laughs, and for voting *His Last Hope* into the position of Christian Small Publisher 2016 Romance Book of the Year. It's been almost a year, and I *still* can't believe it!
- Terri Whitmire and Amy Vanhorn—for working with me to improve my writing. Your feedback has elevated my work, and I thank God for leading me to you both.

SPECIAL MENTION
THE *HIS LAST RESORT* LAUNCH TEAM

Thank you for supporting my writing ministry!
I pray the Lord will continue to bless, keep and use you!

Janine Angel
Ellowyn Bell
Natesha Blanchard
Ann-Tishia Brown-Barnes
Krystina Burke
Kendra Carter
Marsha Cecil
Ardene Cunningham
Denise Daniels
Deborah Dunson
Molly DuParl
Marjorie Foster-Amos
Shana-Kay Fraser
Brandisha Ganzy
Dwayne Gray
Shannan Harper
Cassandra Haywood
Laketha Hicks
Latonya Johnson
Jusilyn Langley
Wanda Laseter

Barrington Lewis
Juanita Miller
Judith Miller
Tanya Mitchell
Lisa Morris
Gail Murray
B. Pierce
Eve Pinkey
Patrice Porter
Marjory Price
Barbara Scott
Marjorie Segree
Michelle Stephens
Sancia Stewart-Williams
Ann Tennie
Monique Toussaint
Hope Townsend
Sonia Walker
Cameisha Williams
Undria Williams
Shelia Young

ABOUT THE AUTHOR

M. A. Malcolm, a native of Jamaica, is a wife, mother, stepmother, daughter, sister and aunt. She is a freelance copy editor, administrative service provider and self-publishing consultant who also works part-time as an educator. With a passion for enhancing the work of Christian writers, she is certified in copyediting and is the founder of Nitpicking with a Purpose (NitpickingwithaPurpose.com). Over the years, she has worked with a host of local and international authors and authors-to-be.

When she published her first book, *His Last Hope: A Contemporary Christian Romance* in July, 2015, she fully expected it to be 'one and done.' She had no intention of writing another book of any kind; however, readers have demanded more, and the Lord has made it possible for her to comply. Not only has He allowed her more time to write; He has also given her more messages to share.

With the publication of *His Last Resort*, the first part of her relatively recent vision of turning *His Last Hope* into a series has come true. She is currently working on two more manuscripts in the series, and has plans for a third.

In 2016, she also became a children's author with the publication of her first children's book, *So very... Max!* – a modern-day response to Hans Christian Andersen's *The Ugly Duckling*.

Mrs. Malcolm has been a part of Faith in Christ Ministries in Westmoreland, Jamaica, for more than ten years. She divides her time among her family; work and writing projects; dogs; to-be-read list, and catching up on much-needed sleep.

She loves hearing from readers, and can be reached via her website authormamalcolm.com. You may also sign up there for her mailing list if you'd like to receive occasional emails and special offers, including free gifts. Book clubs may invite her to appear in person or via the Internet for live discussions surrounding her books. She is also on Facebook and Instagram as @AuthorMAMalcolm.

CPSIA information can be obtained
at www.ICGtesting.com
Printed in the USA
LVOW11s0007080617

537347LV00001B/91/P